MICROBREWED
MURDER

MICROBREWED MURDER

By

Bill Metzger

HOLLISTON, MASSACHUSETTS

MICROBREWED MURDER
Copyright © 2016 by Bill Metzger

Cover Art by Hans Granheim.

First printing February 2016
10 9 8 7 6 5 4 3 2 1

ISBN # 1-60975-135-3
ISBN-13 # 978-1-60975-135-7
LCCN # 2015957698

Silver Leaf Books, LLC
P.O. Box 6460
Holliston, MA 01746
+1-888-823-6450

Visit our web site at www.SilverLeafBooks.com

This novel is dedicated to my friend
Ron Humphreys, who was an inspiration
to me and many others. He died far too young.

MICROBREWED
MURDER

1

I tried to untangle my legs from the twist of sheets and failed; the struggle was more than it was worth to free myself. Trapped, I refocused on the dull pain in my head. I had taken three Advil and drunk a quart of water, but it hadn't taken effect. The amount of beer I'd drunk last night overpowered any attempt to alleviate the hangover.

I remembered the night, at least the first part of it. I'd spent the evening at our newest account, Sweeney's, drinking and buying Nate's beer for people. Attempting to cement a knob, what we said in the business when a bar owner agreed to put one of our beers on tap permanently.

My feet felt cold and I gingerly reached down to pull the Afghan over them, cutting off the draft. Sarah always threw the Afghan over me when I came home late, knowing the blankets would be knocked aside.

Her noise drifted in from the bathroom more loudly than it should have. I burrowed into the tangle I'd made. She was getting ready for work.

Work: the word hit me like a bowling ball, crashing into my brain, scattering my thoughts like pins. There was a lot to do today. Or this week, as Nate would say. He always looked at the big picture. As much of a go-getter as my brother had been, he refused to allow his life to be ruled by the daily tasks.

Random thoughts drifted through my mind like the last few pins. I'd loved that about Nate. He had accomplished so much in his short lifespan. And he'd made it seem effortless. He had the big picture concept. Now that I had taken over the brewery he founded, I realized how gargantuan the effort was.

It was times like this, hung over and unable to marshal my thoughts, that I missed Nate the most. I had never imagined his death would continue to affect me so deeply. In the few years before he had been diagnosed with brain cancer, we had drifted apart, me in my teaching career and marriage and he in his new business. Carry on the tradition of our ancestors, he had always said, who had run a brewery before Prohibition. We stayed in touch over the holidays and family celebrations, but during those years I learned more about my brother from hearing other people talk about him. When they heard my last name, Callahan, they'd ask if I had any relation to the beer. I'd tell them my brother owned the brewery and would hear the stories. Our separate lives had seemed natural.

Nate's success hadn't surprised me. He died young, but had accomplished more than most people do in an entire lifetime. I had always admired—envied, even—my brother's confidence and drive. Now he was gone.

The sound of heels crossing the floor beat a new round of pain into my brain. Next came the perfunctory kiss, followed by the heels signaling their savage departure, a familiar whiff of Sarah's perfume hanging in air. Like the loudness of her heels, Sarah's aroma seemed excessive, an exaggeration brought on by my hangover. A brief thought that I'd forgotten to do something yesterday flitted into my brain. Then the knowledge that she'd leave a note, a To Do list, with chores that needed attention.

Since I'd left the university to take over running the brewery, Sarah and I had developed a new method of communication. There would be no conversation this early with the given that she'd call while on her lunch break at school. I'd find a list next to the coffee maker, which would be loaded and ready.

Unable to return to the welcome armor of sleep, I tried to remember last night. The bar owner, Ian McClaughlin, had appreciated the extra time I'd spent there. He'd been a tough sell. Most Irish pubs were, their loyalty to the local beer distributorship as hard to break as the habits of a sixty year-old beer drinker. But the man had finally agreed to give our beer a try, promising me a knob for the summer. He was Irish, after all, and not afraid of anyone.

I'd celebrated the decision by spending the evening at his pub, moving as much of the first keg as possible through my own system and buying the rest for as many of the pub's locals as would drink it. I was in pain now, but it had been worth it. I imagined fur flying at the next Wehrmann & Sons sales meeting, when they learned that I'd taken one of their knobs. For distributors, the beer business was about control of tap handles. As the final stop before the drinker, knobs ruled. And in this county, Wehrmann & Sons was king. At least that's how Nate had put it. He called them 'The Wehrmacht.'

Nate was born to run a business like this. Besides having it in his blood, he had spent his childhood preparing for it. He was a jock, and once he opened the brewery, he put all the energy he spent on sports fields into his new business. Given the array of sports trophies that lined his den, that was a lot of energy.

The telephone rang in the kitchen and I pulled the blankets over my head, unwilling to move. Sarah couldn't have arrived at school yet and she never turned her phone on in the car. It was probably Stan or Johnny calling from the brewery.

Another facet of Nate's personality was his ability to instill courage in others. To be willing to stand up to the pressures of bigger players, bar owners needed courage. In our case it was Wehrmann & Sons. They were huge, thorough, and frightening. I saw it all the time in bar owners, who while not an easily intimidated group, feared their beer distributor. It went beyond the recognition that they would lose certain benefits; it was a concern for their well being, something that never quite left the business after Prohibition. And while no bar owner I knew had ever been doused, a few had lost their businesses. Since taking over, I had seen too many faces that, when I spoke of replacing a Wehrmann brand for Callahans beer, would reflect panic.

I was drifting again, letting excuses get in the way of sales as Nate would say. Success in the beer business was getting to the owner in the first place and that meant getting around the young flunkies they hired. A few rounds with the twenty -nothings who worked the local bars showed that brewing a great beer, which was what we were all about, was irrelevant. They didn't care about the beer; they were there to make money and meet women. Listening to some old guy talking about his beer was beyond what they were paid to do.

Stan, a partner, my brother's best friend and Callahans' entire sales staff, told me this. He and Nate could mow through the twenty-nothings as easily as the lawns they'd mowed when they were the reigning neighborhood landscape kings. "Lawn Lords" they'd called themselves as teenagers. It was Nate's first business venture and from that time on he'd been hooked.

Nate and Stan had an aggressive confidence, which, when combined with a ledger-like memory of sports trivia, worked wonders with male bartenders. No one knew more about professional sports than Stan, except my brother. His reputation for fact and figure had made him a legend, with his midmorning replays and his assessment of games and whatever they meant to whatever league he was talking about. This news was eagerly awaited by the kids he encountered on his rounds.

Nate also used his age to his advantage; sports history, which he knew from a childhood of poring over box scores and standings, allowed him to compare the day's news with previous sports achievements, making him an awesome purveyor to the faithful. Football, baseball, basketball, hockey—bartenders relied on him to recite play by play the night's events and how they compared to what went before. This was then passed down into sports history that afternoon during their shifts—earning the bartenders a few extra bucks in tips. They had all been at his funeral.

Whether Nate had understood all this or whether he was simply a natural at it, I don't know. He once told me that his real trophies weren't those in his basement, they were the knobs he cemented around town. Every time you saw Callahans beer, you were seeing one of his trophies. It was better than being in his basement, he said, because it was out there for everyone to see.

The phone rang again and I started, realizing that I had dozed off. I felt no better; this was a bad hangover. I lay back, my headache still the number one agenda, even above Sarah's To Do list. The thought crossed my mind that someone might be trying to reach me by cell phone, which was turned off. It wasn't enough to get me up.

That Nate had entrusted his brewery to me was flattering. "It's all I've got, Ed," he'd said, in a rare admission, "and I need you to keep it going." Beyond the pride that he had instilled in me by asking, there were many reasons why I accepted the task. I'd half expected him to sell the business to Stan. "Stan will help," he'd said, "but he needs a leader. You're a leader."

That had surprised me. Nate had always been the leader, the go-getter in the family. From high school and college sports, through his rapid rise in the ranks of corporate sales, to breaking away and investing his money in the brewery, Nate had forged his own path. Yet my brother, this rising star from small town America, had admitted that it would all be for nothing unless I could carry the ball. And expressed confidence that I could. "Don't get too satisfied," he'd told me just before he died. "The moment you feel too satisfied is the moment you begin to die. It means you're letting things happen to you instead of taking it to them." It was just like him to focus on the future, even when he knew he was close to death.

I tried to turn over and felt a wetness on my cheek; even hung over I still couldn't avoid the emotions. I could avoid some things he'd said during his last days, thoughts I didn't even want to fathom nor dwell on beyond that moment when he'd spoken the "Don't get too satisfied" speech. I wasn't entirely sure what he was talking about, but I had been ready for a change. The university job had grown frustrating and Sarah, who had to live with me, thought Nate's passing on the business was a great opportunity.

I also saw a chance to address my weakness. For while my less aggressive, more philosophic nature served me well in the classroom, it was a way to hide insecurity. As if he sensed that, my brother's dying gesture had been to provide me with an opportunity to step out on my own, prove that I could go beyond the ivy tower to run a business.

I tried to get up, but was stopped again by the Afghan tangle. I was surprised at my depth of thought this morning. A hangover of this magnitude usually kept my mind drifting from one random thought to the next, as if the alcohol was impeding the normal transfer of impulses, popping up in random unconnected spots in the brain. Perhaps it was the anniversary of Nate's death, something I had yet to deal with. It had been one year yesterday, another reason I'd drunk too much.

I pushed the memory away, returning to what Nate had considered important, the task. Now that we had captured another knob, the game was on to keep it. Last night's session went a long way toward that and while congratulating myself on the victory, I remembered that I'd have to discuss strategy with Stan. Don't get too satisfied, Nate had said.

The telephone rang again. I decided to get up. I managed to roll off the bed and onto the floor, headed toward the kitchen but too late to stop the answering machine. It kicked in and the message started. It was Johnny, our keg monkey. "Ed, Stan's in the hospital. He was in an accident, Conner's Cliff. It's serious."

2

Hospitals have always seemed antiseptic and impersonal to me, and MacArthur General was no different. The walls were painted a neutral tan as if that was an improvement on gray. White drop ceilings and fluorescent lights portrayed an even greater institutional feel. Posters of medical advice were scattered on walls that also had placards listing the room numbers or directions to different hospital sectors. Perhaps given their sterility, hospitals couldn't help but reflect the fact that they housed so many ill people, I thought. When you were dying, of course, they moved you to a brighter, more upbeat section, as if they wanted your last days to be cheery.

MacArthur General was where Nate had gone for his chemo. The memories weren't pleasant. Only the situation's urgency made me enter; I hadn't visited the hospital since Nate's death.

Stan was in the emergency room, so I wouldn't have to walk the "cheery" halls and recall that futile past. I was relieved to see that Johnny had exaggerated Stan's condition. I could see why; he had been banged up pretty badly. His face must have gone through some glass because it was stitched and bloody. The attendant on duty said he'd recover fully, that between wiring his jaw and some cosmetic surgery he would look like new. He sounded overly optimistic; even with the good news, Stan looked like hell.

My fear that he'd been drunk when he went off the road turned out to be unfounded. Stan had left early last night, letting me handle the celebration, and he'd stopped drinking. So when the officer approached him with a blood alcohol sensor—the doom tube we call it—to take a reading, I stepped between them. Cops were expected to get an alcohol reading after every accident, but they had to ask permission from the "suspect." Since Stan was in no condition to be asked, I was planning to speak for him. I let my company jacket show that I was qualified.

"This wasn't a drinking accident," I said, reading the policeman's name on his badge, Brindisi. My eyes dropped to the device he held in his hand.

Brindisi shook his head. "Has all the hallmarks. Work van, kegs of beer in the back, smells like a brewery."

"Beer sales is his job," I retorted. "Do you think he'd be that stupid to risk losing it?"

"You'd be surprised," Brindisi said.

"At seven in the morning?" I continued, affronted.

"Monday mornings are the second highest drunk driver rate," Brindisi countered. "Sunday evening and people don't want to go back to work."

"Stan loves his work."

"Like I said, you'd be surprised." But he backed off his attempt to dial Stan in, letting the comment hang there.

"Any idea how it happened?" I continued, trying to change the tone of our conversation. It made no sense to anger a guy who was just doing his job.

"They're still investigating," Brindisi replied. "Looks like he missed a curve."

I kept my silence, not wanting to say anything that would sound combative. Especially given that I had already stood him back once. In fact, if anyone had alcohol in his blood it was me and the thought shot through my head that I didn't want Brindisi to know I'd driven to the hospital. But I didn't move, determined not to let him get near Stan. "Can I get your business card?" I finally asked.

Brindisi dug one out of his uniform and handed it to me. Seeing that he wasn't going to get any further, he left the room.

I turned my attention to Stan. He was breathing normally, without assistance. Six months, the attendant had said. How was I going to keep things going without him? A sales guy like Stan, out there talking up our beer, kept us in business. Without him I wasn't sure we could sell what was in our cooler and brite tanks. It was frightening, really, to realize how important he was. This wasn't like the university, where my loss didn't mean much in the grand scheme of things. My sabbatical was inconsequential compared to what Stan's loss would do to Nate's business.

My eyes fell on Johnny, who sat in the corner of the room on his phone. He was a dedicated employee who moved from eskimo to hose dragger to can wrestler with ease, whatever involved moving things around, closing and opening valves and hoses. But he was no Stan; he didn't work well with people.

As if he sensed I was thinking about him, Johnny put his phone away and approached me. "What are we going to do?" he asked.

"You're going to have to take over, Johnny," I replied. "Until Stan heals. We'll react a little slower, but we'll be fine."

He looked relieved. "I told Jenna this morning. Said Stan would be okay. She wanted to know what she could do to help."

"She still in Florida?"

"On her way home. She called from the airport."

Stan's wife was an investor in the brewery. The gossip was that she was once a girlfriend of Nate's, although my brother never admitted it. Just like him to get his former girlfriend to invest in a business he developed. At any rate, Jenna and Stan were a much better fit, two lovebirds who epitomized romance.

"Ed!" Stan's voice made me jump. "Ed!" he repeated in a hoarse whisper, just loud enough for me to hear.

I walked over to the gurney and put my ear close to his lips. "I'm right here, Stan. Relax."

"Keg to Ben..." he whispered but too softly for me to hear.

I put my ear closer to his mouth. "Just relax," I repeated.

"Benson's, Benson's... keg!" he whispered. "Today!"

"I'll take care of it."

"Tap handle!" he whispered hoarsely.

"Right, today." I looked at Johnny. "Stan says we got work to do."

Benson's was a local hangout, a bar that served lunch to an older crowd during the day and turned into a music venue at night. "For the young and the restless," Nate used to say. With the lights off and preparation for lunch already in progress, the place looked dark. I weaved through an array of tables and chairs to the back, where a semi-circular bar gave bartenders the ability to serve a lot of customers. A twenty-nothing was behind the bar, cleaning glasses.

"I'm with Callahans."

"Where's Stan?"

"Accident." I didn't say I was the owner, I had always gauged the service incognito in places that poured our beer, as if I was a normal customer. "Says you ordered a keg of Callahans Copper."

The kid grunted. "Cooler's there. Go through the back door." He pointed vaguely behind him and returned to polishing glassware.

Once I'd driven to the back of the bar, Johnny jumped out and pulled down the tailgate, then unstrapped the can and rolled it along the truck bed to the back. He'd had a lot of practice wrestling cans, full and empty, and handled them well.

Once he'd put the 165 pounds on the dolly, he looked at me. "I think you should try to meet the owner. Stan's been talking about this account for weeks."

"Do you know his name?"

"Nah. But he's probably inside."

I walked back to the cab and grabbed the delivery invoice off the seat. Then headed toward the back door, which the twenty-nothing had left open. Nice of him, I thought, maybe he'd left a trail of bread crumbs to the cooler.

Most of the bars that had started sprouting knobs for all the new beer that was available did it ad hoc, with little thought beyond bringing some in at customer request. A few redid their tap lines and built new coolers, but most just added taps—sometimes towers—to existing space. The bar business worked on significant markups of alcohol, but most owners didn't have a lot of cash to throw around for redesigns. So when it came to keg delivery, the extra kegs they kept in store usually got pushed into the same cooler where they kept the food. This set up a natural conflict between the bartenders and cooks. Usually the owner determined the winner, so it was important to have an owner that valued good beer. It wasn't good to have a can of your beer hanging out in the hallway, or in the heat of a kitchen.

I entered the work space while Johnny muscled the can in. I spotted stairs that looked like they led to a second floor office. As I began climbing them, someone opened the door to the office. I reached the top of the stairs and almost ran into a woman.

"Owner around?"

She shook her head.

I handed her the invoice. "Beer's in the cooler."

"Mo works for you," she replied.

"Our brewer," I said. She looked familiar.

"I know. He's a good friend. I know you, too, Professor Callahan."

I looked at her more closely, recognizing my former student. "Melanie."

"You remember me."

"I remember all my students," I replied a little defensively.

"I convinced the owner to put your beer on tap," she said.

"Well... thank you," I replied, not knowing what else to say. I didn't need to, because she continued without interruption.

"It was a battle. The guy doesn't even know where he's gonna put the line yet, what he's gonna replace. He's got several dogs, but it's like he's afraid to touch 'em. Says it'll piss off one of the regulars."

"What did you tell him?"

"I said tell his regulars that the beer isn't available any longer. That happens all the time, especially with all the merging going on in the import category. *And* I had Stan bring me some samples and gave him a sixer. Nothing like free beer to seal a deal."

"So you gave the guy a Copper," I said, surprised by the level of talk coming from this kid.

She nodded. "And he liked it."

"That's our moneymaker."

"I know."

"What did he think?" I asked, deciding to learn something from her.

"He doesn't know beer, so I mentioned the complex malt profile and balance. I thought I might be losing him so I told him it was local. He *loved* that. Fresh beer, not that shit they ship all the way from Timbuktu."

And promoted by a good-looking woman, I thought. That probably helped the guy make a move to try our brew. It would have moved me.

Melanie continued. "Now we gotta get the owner to pull a knob."

"What's his name?" I asked. Then, embarrassed that I was that unprepared, added, "My sales guy was handling this account."

"Stan."

"Right."

"Owner is Carl Benson. Junior," she added.

"Thanks. Is there anything I can do to help get the beer into the lineup?" I held my breath after asking the question, realizing that I was walking into territory usually left for more experienced players like Nate or Stan. And that this kid would not fall for a bluff answer.

"Stan took care of that already. But he did say he'd get us a tap handle."

"Oh, right. I have that in the pickup, I'll have Johnny bring it in."

"And schedule a Coming Out party."

"Right." Now I was embarrassed. Melanie seemed to know more about the brewery than I did. "Thanks, let me know when you think he'll put it on. By the way, my first name is Ed."

"I know," she replied. "You're Nate's brother. Mo's talked about you. He likes working there. Even with Nate gone and he *loved* Nate."

"Everyone did," I replied.

"Hometown hero," she said. "Anyway, keep making good beer. We're in your corner even if today's customer is not there yet."

On a hunch, I handed her my business card. "We're a small outfit, but if you ever want to sell beer, I could use another sales guy." Then corrected myself. "Person."

"Guy, girl, I'm not offended. I just love good beer. I'm finishing school right now. Only reason I'm here today is we have the week off."

"I understand about school, I've been there," I replied and we both laughed. I turned to leave.

"By the way, we all knew what they did to you. It wasn't fair."

I stopped. "Thanks. For your support, I mean. It meant a lot to me. And if I had wanted to stay and fight, you would have been essential to winning. This opportunity was one I just couldn't pass up."

"No shit," she said. "No one knew at the time why you didn't fight them, but once we heard you were going to take over running a brewery, we all understood. And started drinking only your beer," she added, "at least the committed ones."

I turned back to her. "You know, that's the nicest thing I've heard since leaving those hallowed walls."

"Hallowed my ass, it was a great career move." She grinned and I blushed.

3

I decided to drive past the accident site on the way to the brewery. Johnny hopped back on his cell phone, leaving me time to rethink my view of the twenty-nothings. I was impressed with Melanie and glad she was talking us up at Benson's. She must be a great bartender—knowledgeable about beer and attractive, giving her a receptive audience. You couldn't ask for a better ambassador.

I thought about her comments concerning my fight with the university administration. I hadn't known that any students beyond the few who had helped me do the research—and Melanie wasn't one of them—were concerned. I had made some offhand comments in class, but unless they'd read small bits in the local paper, students wouldn't have known. I wasn't one for taking my fights public, even in this case, where I could have justified such an action. It was a human ecology course, after all. But by the time of the "Fare

-thee-well Conversation" as Sarah called my stormy meeting with our department head, I'd already decided to leave.

Conner's Cliff appeared and I pulled into the space at the other side of the road, before the guard rails, and then considered driving past without stopping. What would I know that traffic investigators didn't? Maybe I could call Officer Brindisi and ask if there had been any progress on the cause of the accident. That was a crazy idea, the guy probably wouldn't even remember me. Worse yet, he'd remember me as the guy who stopped him from doing his job in the hospital emergency room. I got out of the car.

"What are you doing?" Johnny was off his phone.

"Checking out the crash site."

"You ain't gonna find nothin'."

Despite the reportedly high number of accidents happening here, the curve didn't look difficult. Perhaps it was the view that distracted drivers. The road ran along one of the drumlins that characterized the area, rolling hills from a glacial past. The cliff was off a broad curve, well marked with signage from both directions and with enough space before the guard rails to park several cars. Grass grew sparsely due to the constant stopping of sightseers. After that, open space as the land dropped sharply. A guard rail ran along the most dangerous part.

I could see a set of tire tracks leading off the road just before that—only one set. The tracks led to the small embankment where the van must have hit, leaving an empty gash in the undergrowth. Fortunately for Stan, there were no trees nearby and he had been able to avoid the open space and cliff protected by the guard rail. A friend from the Department of Transportation once told me that it was standard procedure to remove trees and any other obstacles that drivers might hit if they drove off the road. They even built road signs so that if a car hit one, the pole would snap instead of acting as an obstacle to passengers. This saved lives, although that safety feature was reserved for the larger road signs, he said.

"I'm gonna cross," I said.

"Look for empties?" Johnny joked. We were always looking for empty cans because losing them was losing money.

I looked both ways and hurried across the road. Johnny was right. I wouldn't find much here. I didn't even know what to look for.

But I did find something. A large piece of broken tail light gleamed red in the grass just off the road's shoulder. I picked it up. It looked new. And not like the tail lights on the van. I scanned the area again. Then walked back across the road, carrying the tail light piece. No cars had passed.

"Hey, who was that chick?" Johnny asked.

"What chick?"

"The one in the bar."

"What bar?"

"Benson's," Johnny said, irritated. I knew what bar Johnny was talking about, but I liked to force him to elaborate beyond his typical one word—or vaguely phrased—comments. It was the teacher in me.

"She's a former student."

"That's right, you used to teach."

"I offered her a job," I said. Then added, "I think she'd be a great sales person."

"A girl?"

"Why not?"

"Sales is a man's job."

"Where have you been for the last generation, Johnny?" I replied, getting into the pickup.

"I know they do a lot of things now, but beer is still a man's game," Johnny said, holding to his point.

"She probably knows more about beer than you do," I replied. He made a face as if to say I was crazy. "Did you know that historically, brewing beer used to be done by the women of the household?" I continued. "That's where the term alewife came from. It was only when it proved profitable and brewing was commercialized that men took over."

"That's what I'm talking about," Johnny replied. "It took men to make it a business."

I started to reply, but stopped.

"I'd do her," Johnny said.

I almost asked him to elaborate, but this was one explanation I could live without. Instead, I replied, "That's probably why you won't." While I knew Johnny would take my response as a criticism, I was being easy on him. I could have mentioned his reputed virginity, so telling in his views on women. I'd also seen the telltale circular imprint of an unused prophylactic that he carried around in his wallet.

"She'd love this," he said, patting his chest. Johnny was proud of his physique and liked to work around the brewery in shorts and a muscle shirt. When he worked in the cold room like that, Mo called him the naked ape. When women came to visit, he often emerged from the back in a muscle shirt. He'd installed a set of weights in a spare room I'd offered him, to work out when he was on break. But despite his bravado, Johnny always fell silent when women were around. Funny thing was, Jenna liked him. I think she felt sorry for him.

I knew Johnny's single-minded approach to muscle building—not his brain power—was why Nate had hired him. That and the fact that he'd been a great tackle guard, one of a younger generation of football players that idolized Nate's high school accomplishments. He was as loyal an employee as we could hope to have.

"She probably won't follow up anyway," I said. "She's still in school and busy." One thing Nate had taught me was that you didn't call sales people. If they didn't call you, they didn't have what it takes to do sales. "But if she does come around," I added, "you'll have to keep your shirt on. She won't be able to handle seeing that body without falling all over you. No work will get done."

Johnny smiled at the softening of my earlier rebuke.

"Let's get lunch."

An hour later, my phone rang. It was the brewery.

"Who left the door open?"

"What do you mean?" I asked. It was Mo.

"I just got here and the door is wide open."

"We'll be there in ten minutes."

❖ ❖ ❖

Most of the microbreweries that had opened around the country were located in business parks with low cost warehouse space or rural areas, where land was cheap. Nate had chosen a building in the city. To no one's surprise, it had once been a brewery. It had gone out of business during the post World War II era of national brand building. We called that time the Bud-Miller-Coors era because when the dust settled, they were the behemoths left standing. Now even the behemoths were being swallowed by larger entities. Nate, who had spent so much time in the corporate world, claimed that as corporations grew, it was as if they couldn't help but gorge on smaller entities until they eventually dropped of their own weight. Then us little guys would start the cycle again.

Callahans Brewery occupied a beautiful brick structure in a decayed neighborhood. The building had to be gutted and rebuilt. Nate had only gotten half way through the master plan before he died, but it had been enough to begin brewing and start bringing in money. I'd brought him the before and after photos just before he died. It was then that I'd promised to finish the job. We were still working on it.

Mo met us at the door. "It was wide open when I got here," he said, giving it a push. We watched it swing open silently. Johnny and I looked at each other.

"I was the last one out," I said. "I'm sure I locked up." I bent down and examined the door jamb. "Hard to tell if it was jimmied. It's looked like this for a while." The door was an old metal one with dents all over it. The door jamb was twisted near the lock, but who could tell when that had happened.

Mo bent down and wiped his finger along the bottom of the threshold, his dreadlocks nearly touching the floor. "Doesn't look like it would take much if they wanted to jimmy it," he said.

"Anything missing?" I asked.

"I don't think so. Beer in the cooler looks good." Mo walked toward the brite tanks as he answered. Nate had often joked that if someone broke into the brewery, they'd probably just steal the beer since that was the only thing of value that would fit through the door.

Motioning Johnny inside, I stepped across the threshold and pushed the door shut. The lock closed after the second push, clicking into place. The dead bolt was another matter. As a habit I locked that, too. "Should we call the police?" I asked.

"What would we tell them?" Johnny replied. "If nothing's missing..."

"They might be able to tell if someone broke in," I interrupted, sounding foolish. 'Excuse me Officer Brindisi, I'm the guy who stopped you from shoving your doom tube into my employee's mouth. I'd like to know if anyone has broken into our brewery.'

Johnny bent down to look at the area around the lock and I realized that we were worse than amateur detectives, standing around examining a door jamb without knowing what to look for.

Mo returned. "Try this." He handed me a tasting glass of a dark, viscous liquid. I smelled it and recoiled. "Wow!"

"Is that bad or what?" Mo said.

"You are the *baddest*," I replied. I set about trying to discern the flavors. Early on I had discovered that my time in the kitchen paid off when tasting beer. Brewers were always experimenting with different flavors and a food lover was more well equipped to discern them. "This one has some nuttiness," I said. I was known for guessing flavors correctly so the pressure was always on to nail them.

"I'm gonna get to work," Johnny said.

"Don't you want some?" Mo asked.

"A Copper," Johnny replied, but he took the small glass that Mo offered him and disappeared into the back.

"How's Stan?" Mo asked.

"He'll be okay."

"What happened?"

"Officer said he went off the road."

"That's not like Stan. He's a good driver."

I didn't reply, nor mention the piece of tail light I'd picked up and left in the pickup. I wasn't ready to pursue that until I spoke with Stan.

"How long will he be out?"

"ER guy said six months, tops."

"I'd say three, knowing Stan," Mo replied. "You taking over his route til then?"

"I don't see that I have a choice. Check this out, the first thing he says to me—he whispers it because he can't even talk yet—is not to forget Benson's. I was awestruck. He's laying there broken and bloody in the Emergency Room and his first concern is that we deliver a keg of beer he promised to one of our accounts. And a tap handle."

"A new account," Mo said.

"Right." I could see why Nate had loved Stan. Together, the two could conquer the world. I put the glass up to my nose again, hopeful that I could capture the secret ingredient. "It's a spice," I said.

"Herb," Mo corrected.

"A spicy herb," I countered.

"True. Do you like it?"

"I do."

"Will it sell?"

"I'm not sure. Maybe in 22s. What stage is it?"

"It's in Oscar," Mo said, indicating the smaller of the horizontal dairy tanks nearby. Like many new breweries, we had scavenged several former dairy tanks to use. Four of them were horizontals, which we'd gone beyond calling sausages, adding nicknames: Oscar, Jimmy, Parks, and Jones. Oscar was the smallest tank. The brite tank, from which we kegged beer, was Johnson. 'Send it to Johnson' meant get the beer ready to put in a keg.

My cell phone rang, but I didn't recognize the number.

"Hello Professor Callahan, this is Melanie."

"Why hello. Are you ready to schedule the Coming Out party?"

"No, I haven't talked to the owner yet. He doesn't get in until this afternoon. I'm calling to take you up on that job offer. I want to know more about it."

"I...I... what about school?"

"The hell with school, I want to do something that involves beer."

"Well, I'm sure we can work something out so that you can finish school," I said.

"I thought you'd say that," she replied. "And that's fine. Maybe an internship."

"I tell you what. I'm having trouble identifying a flavor in Mo's new beer and I think we need your palate. Can you come down?"

"See you in ten," was the reply.

"Melanie?" Mo asked, once I'd hung up.

"She wants to work here," I said.

"I know. She called me this morning all excited that you'd offered her a job. I told her to call you right away as we needed someone. Wasn't sure she'd call."

"What do you think?" I asked.

"She'd be great," Mo said. "She's honest, works hard, and knows beer."

"That's exactly what I thought."

"Imagine having all that in a beer rep."

"Especially knowing beer," I said. The big joke at Callahans was that if our business was based on knowledge of the product, we'd crush the competition no matter how large. Most of the distributors in the business were glorified delivery boys who barely knew how beer was made, not to mention anything about the breweries whose beer they sold. The smart distributors, and there were a few, hired younger kids who knew something. But even the youngsters had to deal with old ways; big businesses like distributorships didn't change quickly. And they were even more reticent because they'd been around so long.

Mo looked at his empty glass. Then at mine. "Beer bitch!" he yelled.

Johnny reappeared, dressed like he was going to the gym—shorts, muscle shirt, white socks, and Nikes.

"What did you think of the beer?"

"Tastes like motor oil." Johnny wasn't big on the experimental side of the beer scene. But he loved the Copper and drank it in copious quantities. We often joked that he consumed a significant percentage of our output. And Johnny could always be depended on to reduce a complex analysis down to its basics, which kept us from over-thinking a beer. Sometimes simplicity was good. One day were all sitting around talking about how to market the Copper and he walked over from the kegging station and without knowing what we were doing, said, "Pop me a Copper." That became our slogan. Simple, direct, and onomatopoeic.

I was about to suggest the herb I was tasting—I thought lemon grass—when the sound of a chair scraping the floor interrupted the silence. We all turned our heads. In all that was going on, I had forgotten the safe, where we kept the small amount of cash on hand, and the recipe books. I rarely locked it.

"Did you check the office?" I asked Mo. His face told me that he hadn't.

Johnny was the first one to move toward the noise.

4

"Johnny, stop!"

He was halfway across the office, closing in on the intruder, when he froze. Having seen Johnny's explosive side at football games, I was surprised that he could stop. Until I realized who had yelled; Jenna sat in the chair behind my desk. Across the room, in Johnny's path, sat the intruder, in a hospital gown.

"Stan!" I yelled. Stan lifted his arm as if to greet us, then set it down, grimacing. The hospital gown brought the memory back: Nate doing the same thing, busting out of the hospital rather than languishing there. He'd had help and that help sat in a wheelchair just like he had months ago. If I wasn't so surprised, I would have been spooked at the similarities.

"I thought you said he was all banged up." Mo interrupted my thoughts. Stan looked ghastly. His head was covered with bandages and one arm was in a sling.

"Deliver Benson keg?" Stan whispered.

"Of course," I said. "We just got back."

He was about to continue, but Jenna interrupted. "Stan, that's enough. Now let's go." She stood and walked over to him. "I'm sorry guys, he insisted that I bring him here against my better judgment. He wouldn't tell me why until now: so he can give you his delivery list in person. It's on the desk." She leaned close to Stan's non-bandaged ear. "I could have done this and you wouldn't have almost gotten clobbered by Flannery High's best linebacker." She glanced at Johnny, who stood with his arms at his sides as if uncertain what to do with them. "Thanks for listening, Johnny. At least someone does."

"Good you were here," Mo said.

"I wish he had told me what was so important," Jenna replied, still sounding miffed.

I thought about what had happened. Stan's dedication for success was close to obsession. Leaving the hospital on the day you're admitted to the Emergency Room isn't normal behavior, not in Stan's condition. He was acting just like Nate. Maybe it was something else. Maybe Stan knew something. "Is everything okay at the hospital?" I asked, suddenly worried.

"Everything is fine!" Jenna replied. "Except that he shouldn't move around like this." Stan shrugged. "Stubborn!" Jenna added. She unlocked the wheels.

"You're the best, babe," he said weakly as she began to push him.

"Can I help?" Johnny asked.

"He's not that heavy," Jenna replied.

"How did he get you to bring him here, anyway?" Mo asked.

"I was given an order I couldn't refuse."

I smiled. While that sounded odd given the situation, it was pure Stan and Jenna. I remembered Stan saying the same thing when he decided to work for Nate. He had given up a local golf pro job, one all his friends envied. When I asked him why he'd decided to take such a risk, I thought he would say he needed something with more action. Instead, he used the same words Jenna had: "I was given an order I couldn't refuse." He'd wanted to work for Nate all along, but Jenna's "order" was the confirmation he needed. Likewise, Stan's "order" had pushed her to bring him to the office. The two were crazy in love.

As they reached the door, I said, "Stan, one thing before you go. Do you remember what happened?" He didn't reply. "The accident. How you went off the road," I prodded.

"Bump," he said.

"Did you hit a bump or get bumped?"

Stan didn't answer and Jenna turned. "He's pretty drugged up. I'm surprised he remembers who I am."

I suddenly felt very tired.

Melanie arrived shortly after Jenna and Stan had gone. "Was that *Stan*?" she asked, her voice displaying the reverence that many held for Callahans' main man.

"None other," Mo replied.

"I thought he was in the hospital."

"So did we," I said.

"Iron man," Mo said.

Johnny had already disappeared and Mo went to get more samples of his latest brew. I beckoned Melanie into the office. Once we'd discovered that the intruder was Stan, I didn't bother to check the safe. I briefly explained to Melanie the multitude of tasks behind the job she'd signed on for and the amount of pay, which wasn't much considering the work load. I wasn't accustomed to hiring people so I told Melanie what I knew about the bar and store owners we dealt with and how and when we usually delivered. She suggested a few bars that were not on Stan's list, indicating a good knowledge of our market.

Mo returned and handed glasses around. "Lemon grass," Melanie said.

"That's my girl," Mo confirmed and I knew I'd made the right move to hire her.

"My parents are foodies," she said modestly.

We discussed the beer's possibilities. Amazingly, the flavors worked. The spice balanced out the roast flavor of the black malts. A slight sweetness left over from the base malt blended the combination well and hid the higher alcohol level. The beer was new so while the spice seemed a little harsh, a little time would allow it to evolve, giving it a more nuanced overall character.

The big question, of course, was if it would sell. Mo was a renaissance man, pushing the envelope and something this daring would challenge even today's beer lovers. We could always push it into the seasonal category; cold weather was several months away and Mo's spicy stout would have some time to mature. The timing seemed right.

I picked up Stan's list and looked it over. There were seventeen kegs to be delivered. "We have some catching up to do," I said.

"I can help," Melanie said quickly. "You can explain more about the job to me."

"That would be great."

"You look tired, Professor Callahan."

"Ed," I said, "call me Ed."

"I'll try," she promised.

Mo looked over my shoulder at the list. "She's right. You can deliver all those tomorrow."

I looked at him, grateful. Then at Melanie. "Can you meet me here tomorrow morning, early?"

"What time is early?"

"Seven," I replied. "That way we can go over a few things before heading out. Also, that will give us more time. We can't work as fast as Stan."

She looked at her watch. "I'll be here. Right now I plan to go back to Benson's and make sure the Copper gets put on tap."

Minutes after Melanie left, Johnny emerged. "Where'd she go?" he asked.

"Who?" Mo asked.

"The girl."

"What girl?"

"The one Ed's gonna hire. You know."

"She's hiding," Mo said. "We warned her about you."

"Right," Johnny said. He glanced at his biceps.

"Melanie left," I said. "I'll introduce you tomorrow. But you have to promise to dress appropriately. I don't want her changing her mind."

It wasn't until I was on my way home that I remembered the broken piece of tail light. I glanced back at the rear seat, suddenly afraid that it might have disappeared. It lay where I'd left it. I wondered if my suspicions were far-fetched and decided to run them past Sarah when I got home. She would help me evaluate what I thought, which until this point seemed anecdotal.

Sarah met me with hot chile soup, the best hangover remedy I knew. I sat down at the kitchen table and waited while she dished some into a bowl.

"How's Stan?" She had listened to the messages on the answering machine and wanted to know more. She set the bowl of soup in front of me and as I ate, I briefed her. I ate slowly, savoring the burn, knowing its healing effects.

"And how are *you*?" she asked once I finished describing Stan's injuries. She kissed the top of my head.

"Tired." I told her about Stan showing up at the brewery later that day.

"He couldn't have been that badly hurt," she replied. "He wouldn't have been able to move that much."

"I think he looks a lot worse than he is, if you're counting broken bones and contusions." I finished the soup and decided not to mention my suspicions. I was too tired to go through the analytical process behind my thoughts and knew that Sarah would take me there. She was my best critic. Right now I just wanted to sleep.

5

The next morning I awoke early and made coffee for Sarah while she showered. The aroma of the espresso met her as she stepped out of the hot, steamy bathroom. She took it and kissed me. Then lingered over the drink while I made one for myself.

"What time is dinner?"

"Hard to tell," I replied. "I'm breaking in a new sales person. I thought I'd take her around to Stan's accounts since I have to drop off beer."

"Her?" she asked.

"Melanie. I met her at Benson's. She's a former student."

"So you're back to dating students," Sarah teased.

"I was thinking … our relationship has grown boring again," I retorted, pulling her to where I was seated and laying my face against her stomach. We had played this jealousy game—me dating students and she teachers—for years.

The playful accusations helped keep things lively and helped relieve the unfounded suspicions that arose in any long term relationship. We were too happy to cheat on each other. At least I was.

"You want boring," Sarah replied, "I'll show you boring. Be here for dinner at six."

"How about right now?" I reached inside the towel and ran my hand up her thigh.

She moved away. "You had your chance last night. You were out like a light."

"Sorry," I said. "It was a long day."

"You owe me." She set her coffee mug down in the sink. "Can't be late for work." The towel dropped off her as she disappeared into the bedroom and I whistled. Sarah's body, "lumps and bumps" as she described herself, was sexy to me even so many years later.

I always reminded myself how lucky we were. We had managed to navigate the narrows of faith and fidelity in our marriage for over ten years. Sure there were disappointments and moments of boredom and frustration, but we were still together and content, while couples around us split like amoebae. Each staff get-together, whether at the university or at the schools where Sarah worked, revealed another rocky or wrecked marriage. Sometime the trysts we discovered made our monogamy seem the odd one, but in them I mostly saw unfulfilled longing. As Sarah said, they were far better at communicating to one of us than to their partners.

❖ ❖ ❖

Melanie was waiting when I arrived. She was wearing a skirt and shoes with heels. Not too overdressed for sales but no good for can wrestling. On the positive side, she wore little makeup and no perfume, vanities you didn't see much of in the brewing industry. I apologized for not telling her to dress for deliveries.

"That's okay," she said. "I wasn't sure, so I brought work clothes, too. I'll get them out of my car."

"You can change inside while I get the paperwork." I opened the door, then turned. "Johnny hasn't come yet, has he?" I worried about Melanie changing in the back room.

"I haven't seen anyone and I've been here fifteen minutes."

"And the door was locked when you got here?"

"Yeah."

I waited for Melanie to enter and closed the door, remembering the concern it had caused me yesterday. Having Stan out of the lineup was bad enough; a break-in would have been a worse blow. But the worries were unfounded. With Mo and Johnny, I had a good team and I expected Melanie was in that same mold. She showed up at the door with a small backpack. "Back behind the sausages is a bathroom," I said, pointing toward the dairy tanks.

I entered the office. Stan's delivery book lay on my desk. Next to it was the broken piece of tail light. I didn't remember putting it there. Had I grabbed it out of the pickup yesterday? I might have done that automatically and not remembered, given all the confusion. My suspicions rose again. Was it actually the van's tail light? It looked different.

And hadn't I left it in the pickup? Was this some sort of warning? I had been too tired to run my suspicions past Sarah last night and she hadn't had time this morning. I picked up the piece of plastic and wondered if it was important or a symptom of some deeper insecurity.

I heard noise in the back and thought of Melanie changing. It was a nice image. She had a body shape like Sarah's. I thought about all the times I'd lain in bed while Sarah took her clothes off and anticipation grew. When we dined out, she would ask me how she looked. I always told her she looked better without the clothes. I felt lucky.

The back door opened and I jumped. "Johnny!" I yelled, startled. I stepped to the door where I could see him. "Come here!"

He looked at me as if I was crazy, then said, "Let me put my shit away."

"No, right away," I insisted. "I need you!"

He ambled over and I waited, relieved that I'd steered him away from where Melanie was.

"What's up?"

"Can you look that over and give me the best route to travel?" I pointed to Stan's list, which lay on my desk.

"That can't wait?" he asked, looking surprised.

"I want to get going right away."

He grabbed the list. "Who's car's out there?" At that moment, Melanie walked in. She looked stunning; jeans, a cream orange, three quarter sleeve shirt, and a pair of work shoes was all it took.

"Wha…" Johnny began.

"You remember Melanie from Benson's," I said. "She's our new sales woman. Melanie, this is Johnny."

"Hi," she said, reaching out to shake Johnny's hand. He took her hand and shook it gently, and I knew he was a goner. The funny thing about Johnny was that for all his macho talk about women, if he liked you, he was overly meek. It was a Jekyll and Hyde thing.

"Let me see that list," I said, holding out my hand. "I changed my mind, want to try out my new GPS. We won't need directions."

"Welcome aboard," Johnny said, handing me the list but keeping his eyes on Melanie.

"Thank you," Melanie replied. "I hope I can live up to the high standards you guys have set for Callahans."

"If you need any help with anything, let me know," Johnny replied. "I'm a pretty good mechanic, too, if you have any car problems."

"Can you help us load the cans?" I asked, wanting to get things moving before he embarrassed himself into offering to change the oil in her car. I'd seen him do that before with a woman he liked.

"Let me change," Johnny said.

"Nice guy," Melanie said once he'd left.

I nodded, laughing inwardly at the difference in his approach since yesterday. I bet myself he'd show up to help us with a shirt on this morning.

❖ ❖ ❖

I shouldn't have worried about Melanie's ability to wrestle cans; she didn't let her feminine side get in the way of manual labor. At each stop, she pushed me to go into the bar and "do business" while she took the can off the pickup and wheeled it in. She was quiet and efficient, collecting the empties after dropping off the full kegs. If I was able to get anyone's ear, she used the time to mark our progress on the drop-off list.

Melanie got more than one look from the twenty-nothings who sometimes met us at the back door. A couple of them even asked who she was and I used it to my advantage, telling them that I was considering giving her full time work if I could build up the business. If Nate could use the sports angle to win over customers, I could use a pretty woman.

It worked. Several times I was led to a decision maker who ordered kegs of our seasonal. I promised I'd have Melanie deliver them later that month, when the beer was ready.

Between drop-offs Melanie related how she had become interested in beer. She'd had a boyfriend in the business. She'd left him, but not her love of beer. And not just drinking it. The entire business, from brewing to distribution to retailing excited her. The small, independent business model that microbreweries were based around was inspirational.

I knew what she meant. Since the 1980s, the brewing industry had been revolutionized. People who bore nothing more than a love of good beer, many from having brewed it at home, had entered this business. These newcomers had focused on quality, creativity, and camaraderie—the last trait being necessary with small startups trying to break into an industry ruled by giant companies. Our fight was against those companies, which were brewing what Mo called "penguin beer," spending their money on marketing campaigns and back room deals.

What had emerged from the micro-brewing side of the industry was exciting, and Nate had bought into it. Instead of following a path up the corporate ladder, he had saved his money to buy a building in the heart of downtown, rebuilt it with his own hands, and found a brewer. Stan was the genius behind the reconstruction. Their story was familiar in this industry, and rung back to the days of a bygone American era. While the brewing business was far from one that brought riches, the two of them had built something sustainable, and were doing what they loved.

Our delivery route took us past Benson's. "What about that keg you delivered?" I asked, reminded that Melanie had said she was returning there yesterday.

"He's all set. Coming Out party this Thursday."

"You ever been to a Coming Out party?"

"Never," she admitted. "But I've heard about them."

The DrinkUps! had been Nate's idea. Each time a bar gave us a knob, we offered a little party and our staff and all the friends and family we could muster showed up to celebrate. When Nate had been around, we had worn suits and ties, as if attending a formal. Later, under Mo's inspiration, we began to wear more outlandish outfits. For me that simply meant a brightly colored Hawaiian shirt, but Mo had gone all out, wearing anything from traditional African garb to bearskin pants and coat. He looked marvelous, his dreadlocks cascading down the back of a full armor of fur. The irony, of course, was that Mo was a vegetarian. He didn't hesitate to give us a lecture on the perils of meat eating, but justified his bear coat by claiming it had been handed down to him by ancestors who stretched back to pioneer days.

The DrinkUps! brought us a lot of attention, and new business. They also gave us the elusive cachet that every business hoped would translate into greater sales. The parties were a great way to excite people about a new local business. "They come for the gear and stay for the beer," Mo boasted. Johnny, of course, stuck to his shorts and muscle shirt.

6

It wasn't until just before our last stop that Melanie spotted the broken tail light. She had turned around to look at the bed of the pickup, filled mostly with empty cans. "Look at that! Only two kegs left!"

"Fantastic!" I replied.

"What's this?" She picked the tail light off the back seat and held it in her hand. "Did you back into someone?"

"That's not from my car," I said defensively, at the same time wondering how the hell the tail light had made it back into the car. Were there two of them?

"Looks like a truck tail light, or turn signal light," she said.

"That's what I thought when I first saw it. It was at the scene of the accident."

"What accident?"

"Stan's, where he went off the road. But it's not from our van."

"Whose is it?"

"I don't know," I replied. She was about to put the tail light back where she had found it when I decided to tell her the whole story. I started at the hospital scene after Stan's accident and ended with my suspicions about Wehrmann & Sons. Stan would never have gone off the road without help, I explained, and I knew he'd had run-ins with the local distributor. As I related my suspicions, they began to sound far-fetched. I could hear Sarah asking me why such a big company would bother with us. She'd say we probably weren't even on their radar. I finished sheepishly, telling Melanie I'd returned to the site of Stan's accident and found the piece of tail light. For some reason, I thought it might give me a clue as to what had happened.

To my surprise, Melanie thought my suspicions were credible. "Have you spoken to anyone there?" she asked.

"Where?"

"Wehrmann & Sons."

"I don't know anyone."

"Do you have to?"

"Well, to tell the truth, I'm not convinced that this isn't just paranoia," I replied. "I did start a conversation with the policeman who was at the hospital where they'd taken Stan. I haven't…"

"Did you look at the va…here, take a left!" she suddenly said. I turned without signaling, earning a loud horn from the driver behind me.

"He shouldn't be tailing you anyway," she said.

"This isn't the way to the garage." I noticed we were driving along an industrial park area.

"What garage?" Melanie asked.

"Where the van is."

"We're not going there. We're going to the source."

Wehrmann & Sons was located in the outskirts of an upscale area outside the city. Taxes had been low when they built, but the expanding suburbs had caught up with them. Over that time, and with the help of numerous other industries, they had managed to make the area look upscale as well. The beer distributor's building was on a wide asphalt road divided by a grassy berm that was cut and polished like a manicure. Ornamental plants and the occasional tree dotted the berm.

"Park in there," Melanie commanded, pointing to a driveway entrance. "You can't go through the gate without alerting security. The delivery trucks are in the back."

I did as she asked. "You sound like you know this place."

"Follow me!" she said, grabbing the tail light. I leapt out after her.

She entered the warehouse through a small side door. Inside lay signs, portable coolers, boxes of glasses and coasters, and more beer marketing materials neatly arranged and within easy reach. There was even an outdoor grill. A large overhead bay door was next to the door where we entered. A fork lift was parked nearby.

"Let's move quickly," she said. "They have cameras." She pointed to the upper far corner of the room where a camera gaped at us.

I followed her toward the back of the building, through a second, larger warehouse area filled with tiers of easily accessible shelves that held cases of beer. There were dozens of brands from dozens of breweries. I knew most of the brands, had seen them on the knobs sprouting around town. Competitors.

"Control," Melanie commented as she walked toward the back. I raced to keep up with her.

"What are you doing here?" The voice came from in front of Melanie, bringing her up short.

"I'm looking for George," she replied.

"Who let you in?" It was a uniformed security guard.

"I'm looking for George," Melanie repeated.

"You're going to have to go back through the office," the guard said. I noticed that he wasn't carrying a weapon.

"Tell George I want to see him," Melanie said. "I'll meet him out back." She slipped past the guard and out the back door. The guard made a move to follow her, unsure of himself. "Tell him Melanie is here," she called as the door closed.

I looked at the guard and shrugged. "You call George and I'll keep track of her," I said. The guard grabbed the walkie-talkie on his belt.

Outside, a huge asphalt parking lot was surrounded by a six foot high chain link fence. The lot harbored only a few trucks. "Not the greatest timing," Melanie said. "They're still out on deliveries. But let's look anyway." She walked quickly to the back end of the trucks and scanned them. I ran along the front, thinking suddenly that if Stan had been pushed off the road, it would have been a front end turn signal that would have broken, not a tail light.

"Why hell-oohh..." An average build man in a suit and tie was standing just outside the door. He looked at the security guard and nodded. The guard left.

"George," Melanie said unemotionally and walked toward him. He opened his arms and pulled her in, giving her a big kiss. She averted his lips, I noticed, but he held her longer than seemed warranted for a casual relationship. "Mmmm... I miss that!" he purred. "Are you ready to come back?" Melanie broke free.

He looked at me. "Who's this old man?"

"Ed Callahan," she said.

"Oh," he replied. "I'm just glad you didn't say he was your boyfriend. He's old enough to be your father." I felt like replying that the same could be said of him. Despite his business suit and shiny black shoes, he looked and spoke like he'd spent decades making shady deals in back rooms. Sleazy.

I stretched out my hand. "Ed Callahan. Callahans Brewery."

That got his attention. "Oh yeah. You're the one who decided to go it alone."

"My brother did," I corrected him.

"You could have been with us." His arm swept around him, as if to indicate the grandness of the business he owned. Or was it his daddy? No one knew the financial details.

"Are you missing this?" Melanie held up the tail light piece.

If George knew anything about what Melanie held in her hand, his eyes didn't reveal it. They were slitted—crocodile eyes, I thought—and didn't move a bit. He didn't even reply, just shrugged.

"We were wondering if it came off one of your trucks," Melanie bravely forged on.

"I wouldn't really know," George finally responded. "Tony takes care of the vehicles."

"Ask him," she said.

"Have you decided to come back to me?" George asked again.

"Give me a week." I could see in George's face that her reply was a rebuff.

"I might be gone," he finally said.

"I'll tell you what," she said. "Get back to me about whether any of your trucks are missing a tail light cover and I'll think about it. Ask Tony. Let's go Ed."

"Who's Tony?" I finally asked as we left our last keg drop. We had done the last couple drops in silence. Melanie was obviously upset from the visit to Wehrmann & Sons and I respected her need for silence. In some ways I felt responsible for bringing it on, and didn't know what to say.

"Tony is George's brother," she said. "He's the crazy one. You'll know what I mean when you meet him."

"One is enough for today," I replied. "I feel like I just emerged from an oil slick."

"I can't believe I dated him!" she said, a note of anger in her voice.

"Sorry I..."

"Don't be," she interrupted. "Oil's a pretty accurate assessment."

"He's a lot older than you," I said. "He must be..."

"Ten years," she interrupted. "That was a lot at my age." For a minute I thought she was going to cry.

I waited a few moments, then said, "We all make mistakes. And not only when we're young."

"He taught me a lot," she said. "About sex, anyway, he was good at that. But not much about love." I remained silent, a little embarrassed that Melanie was revealing this to me. "Asshole," she finished.

"It helps when love and sex go together," I said, realizing how dumb that sounded. Then decided to change the subject. "Nate thought they were all assholes. They came to him with a lowball offer for his beer and he rejected it out of hand. They came back higher—still too low of course—saying that was a standard part of the negotiations but to Nate it was an insult. And the death knell of ever doing business with them."

"So that's why Barrels is with Wehrmann and you're not?"

"More or less." Barrels was the other local brewery, a competitor. At the time, they were a couple of home brewers wanting to make it big. Now they had knobs all over town.

Mo thought the beer sucked and always made fun of their marketing slogan "German Beer Made in America," saying the brewery wouldn't have lasted six days in Germany, where most breweries had existed for hundreds of years.

"Were you able to get anything out of his reaction?" I asked.

"George doesn't react," she said. "He digests."

The picture of a snake immobile while the mouse it just swallowed is slowly broken down into food popped into my head. That was George.

"But whatever he does or doesn't do, he's been warned that we're watching him. He does react to that."

"I didn't mean to bring you into this," I replied. "It's not exactly part of sales."

"Don't worry," Melanie replied. "A visit to that place... actually it helped me realize what a fool I was. How could I *ever* have dated him!" she repeated.

"Well I'm glad to have helped your personal life," I joked. "No charge for the consultation."

"We're even," she said.

I looked at my watch. It was 6:15. I was late for dinner.

7

I hadn't expected to see Officer Brindisi again, especially at Benson's. He was there for a monthly get-together of police officers and fire fighters, Guns and Hoses Night. The bar owners I'd met weren't particularly skilled at scheduling events, but this time the double booking boosted the crowd for our Coming Out party.

"Pop you a Copper?" Every time I made that offer I remembered the discussions over the marketing slogan for Callahans first bottled product, Copper. The original idea, "Pop a Copper!" had been Johnny's, but Nate hadn't liked the negative connotations. "Buy you a Copper?" had won out officially, but Johnny's choice—in an industry that welcomed edgy—had taken over, even after all of the marketing materials had been purchased.

Brindisi looked at me. "You're the guy from the hospital."

"Right," I said. "Just protecting my staff. Sorry."

"I don't like that part of the job either," he said. "It's required."

"I understand." I tried to make the conversation lighter, held up my beer and added, "I'm not driving tonight." He laughed. "Any more on the accident?" I asked.

Brindisi's eyes narrowed. I continued. "My guy went off the road at Conner's Cliff."

"He should feel lucky to be alive; that's a dangerous corner."

"I was at the accident site that same day and found a broken piece of a turn signal casing."

"We're not in the habit of picking up pieces of your car," Brindisi replied, souring a little.

"It wasn't ours."

"What are you saying?"

"Could another car have forced my guy off the road?"

"You should ask your guy that."

"I did. He doesn't remember. Said he hit a bump, but there aren't any bumps in the road there."

"Do you have reason to believe someone would force your guy off the road?" Brindisi asked. He sounded like an assistant DA. I shrugged and he added, "An angry girlfriend? A girlfriend's husband? Someone he doesn't want to talk about?"

"His wife was in Florida. And they're happily married."

"Piece of turn signal could be anyone's," Brindisi continued. "That turn has seen a lot of accidents."

"Any lately?"

"I wouldn't know."

"The piece was brand new. Any way of checking on accidents there?"

"If it was reported," Brindisi replied. "But a lot of accidents never are. Especially with no injuries."

"It just seems too coincidental." The bartender put the beers down and turned to get me a tray to carry them to the table.

"I'm not sure what you're implying," Brindisi said.

"I don't know either," I replied. "It's just that Stan is a good driver. An accident seems unlikely."

"Stan the one they pulled out of the van?"

"Right. That doesn't happen to a guy like him."

"With cell phones, it happens more than you'd think."

I decided not to continue the conversation. My suspicions were beginning to sound far-fetched again and I could see Brindisi wanted to return to his friends. "Let me know what you think of the beer. We're celebrating the Copper tonight, first time on tap." He hesitated, and I added, "It's made locally."

"Sure," Brindisi said, and left. I felt like he was doing me a favor by trying it, that he was a loyal big brand drinker. Another penguin. It was an image the beer snobs in the industry savored, the masses of big brewery drinkers following the penguin in front of them, unlike those of us who wanted flavor in our beer.

Before I left the bar I noticed a business card near my beer. It was Brindisi's. I slipped it into my pocket and headed back to our table. It never hurt to have two.

Benson's was split into two rooms. The bar was in the front, probably the original room, opened long ago. A large arched passage led into a second, more modern room where we were sitting. The middle of the second room was a large area, the middle of which was filled with the officers, who had pushed together enough of the tables to fit their group. The lighting was just good enough to read a menu. Two televisions glared from opposite corners; the sound was off and a different game was on each. It was basketball and hockey season, I noticed.

"What was that all about?" Melanie asked, once I'd returned. She sat with Mo and Johnny.

"He's the officer who tried to shove a doom tube down Stan's throat in the hospital," Johnny replied.

"He's okay," I added, wanting to avoid bad feelings.

"Place is packed," Johnny commented.

"Guns & Hoses." Mo motioned toward the group of officers.

Melanie sat up suddenly. "Don't look now, but the Wehrmann brothers just came in."

"Looks like they brought the whole family," Johnny added.

I turned around. Despite the large crowd already in the bar, the entry of the Wehrmann & Sons staff was noticeable. At the head was George. Another, larger, more muscular man was next to him.

"That's Tony," Melanie said, her face betraying no emotion.

"Looks mean," I said.

"Too bad there's no place for them to sit," said Johnny, his voice betraying satisfaction.

"They won't sit," Melanie said. "They'll squeeze into a position at the bar, nearest the door. Several of the reps had already worked themselves into a spot at the bar, easing aside customers that hadn't claimed a bar stool. The spot became the central point from which George and Tony reigned.

"A lot of 'em," Mo said.

"Beer reps, delivery guys, office clerks, you name it," Melanie added.

Once George reached the bar he ordered a round of Barrels Pilsners.

"Once that keg kicks, our seasonal beer goes on," Melanie said. "A second tap."

"Won't that be surprising," Johnny said gleefully.

"Won't happen," Mo said.

"What do you mean?" I asked.

"Owner doesn't have the balls. He'll wait until he can do it without the Wehrmanns in front of him."

"It'll happen," Melanie said confidently.

I never thought watching a beer spout pour could be so tense, but I couldn't keep myself from glancing over each time the bartender poured one of the dozen or so pints George Wehrmann had ordered. I wasn't sure if I wanted to see the cough and spit of a kicked keg and the resulting moment of truth.

"Marv is still with them," Johnny observed.

"Who's that?" Mo asked.

"The one on the end with the red shirt. Used to work for us," Johnny explained. Johnny had been with Nate from the beginning. Mo had been brought in later, when Nate needed help brewing.

"Traitor," Johnny said.

"He bought the E-Z Pass." Mo had a way with words that reminded me of Nate.

"Health insurance got Marv," I said. When Nate first opened Callahans, he'd been unable to afford health insurance for staff. Wehrmann & Sons had a well established benefits package, so Marv had walked. "You can't blame him." I added.

"He orders the same beer every time he's here. Barrels Pilsner," Melanie said.

"He's tasting the beer, but drinking the Kool-Aid," Mo added. We'd all heard that one before. Too many sales reps drank only the products their company distributed. That wasn't difficult here given the large number of knobs the Wehrmanns controlled around town. And in Marv's case it was supportive of his employer. But it also meant that he didn't know beer as well as he should. Nate had insisted that his employees try beers beyond his own. Full pints, not just the samples that had become common to ask for in the industry. The microbrewery industry was not one that promoted loyalty to one brand; there were too many flavors out there to try and its beer drinkers were more concerned with taste than the penguins.

Melanie stood up and walked to the table of police and firemen.

"What's she doing?" I asked.

"Buying them a round," Johnny said. Once things got going at a Coming Out party, we would go to each table and offer a free pint of our beer to anyone who wanted one.

"Well schooled," Mo observed, echoing my thoughts. This was supposed to be my job yet I had been diverted, first by Brindisi, then the arrival of the Wehrmann crowd.

Melanie got a round of orders and went to the bar to order them. The bartender gave her immediate service. I noticed that she stayed away from George.

I was so involved in watching my new sales person interact with the bar patrons that I didn't notice the keg of Barrels Pilsner kick. She did, and when the knob started kicking foam she handed the tray to one of the officers and walked back to the bar. The bartender, a twenty-nothing whose attention she obviously commanded, passed by her on the way to the cellar. I saw him nod. When he reappeared, he pulled the knob again, until the liquid from the replaced keg began to run. He pulled four pints and brought them to Melanie. She brought them to our table and the bartender returned to the Wehrmann sales reps.

Mo looked at the beer in the glass. It was dark, not Barrels Pilsner.

"What did you say?" I asked.

"I told him where I'd left the tap handle for our seasonal," she said. "Told him where to look in the back room. He didn't have to."

"Smooth," Mo said.

"He your boyfriend?" Johnny asked.

Melanie blushed, but didn't say anything.

"Really, Johnny, get a grip," Mo said.

"I was just asking," Johnny said. "I don't want to have to fight off jealous boyfriends for sitting here."

"Melanie doesn't need a private guard when she commands the regiment," Mo replied. "Even the older guys do what she wants around here if you hadn't noticed."

While this conversation happened, I watched the bar. The bartender had returned to the Wehrmann crowd and shrugged off their protests about the change of beers. They ordered something different, another of the Wehrmann knobs, and let it go at that. But George had realized for the first time that Melanie was here. At least that's what I thought he saw; I doubt he recognized me after our brief encounter. He picked up his beer and approached our table. Tony followed him.

Johnny leaned back in his chair, the front two legs leaving the floor to open up a little more space near the two brothers. To my surprise, George directed his comments to me, completely ignoring Melanie. "I had the trucks checked," he said. "No damage to any of them. I wanted you to be the first to know."

"Thanks," I replied, surprised again, this time by the gist of his words.

"That's a tight corner for those who don't know how to drive a heavy load," he added. "You wouldn't be the first one to lose a truck there." I was about to reply that Stan was a good driver, when he continued. "Nice job getting your beer on tap here."

"Owner wants some diversity," I replied, wanting to keep the conversation away from Melanie, for her sake.

"We got more diversity than anyone in the state," he said, keeping his voice even.

"Maybe it's the local thing, then," I said.

"Well, don't think we won't try to take that knob back when the season changes," George said.

"Fair enough." I looked him in the eyes, my thoughts buried behind a frozen smile. Just another student with a dumb comment, I told myself. Over the years I'd learned how to disguise my disappointment when it wouldn't elicit further information.

As George turned to go, Tony fixed his gaze on Melanie. Still gazing at her, he said to his brother. "Isn't this the kid you were bangin'?"

Johnny moved before anyone knew what was happening. The chair legs slapped down on the floor and his shoulder came up quickly, connecting with Tony just below the rib cage. I could hear the solid hit, and wind driven out of lungs that sounded like the cough of an old man too weak to muster up harshness. Tony fell on his ass. He looked up in disbelief as Johnny sat back down.

"Don't insult her," Johnny said as tough boy gasped for air.

Several of the Wehrmann's sales team approached once they realized what had happened. They formed a semi circle around Johnny, as if well rehearsed. I looked at my team, expecting trouble. We'd get the worst of it. But the police officers had heard the commotion and before anything went further, they swarmed the area. Reputations aside, most police prefer the role of peace keepers and this group was not about to let a fight spoil their night out.

George was the first to speak. "Help him up," he said to a couple of his employees, who jumped to Tony's side. He waved them away and stood. Unable to speak, his eyes sent a warning before he turned away.

"Peace," Mo said, and the word hung there like a tee shirt left to dry when the rest of the laundry had been taken down.

The Wehrmanns and their sales reps returned to the bar en masse.

"Sorry," Johnny said, looking at Melanie. "I couldn't let that one pass."

"Once a linebacker, always a linebacker," Mo observed.

Melanie was the first to see the blood trickling from the side of Johnny's head.

8

At this point I was inclined to let things lie. Johnny had humiliated Tony Wehrmann in front of his entire staff. Thanks to the police presence the situation hadn't gotten out of control, but I wondered if word of the incident would get back to the owner. Bar owners found plenty of reasons for changing knobs and there was no use giving him another. I planned to send Melanie to Benson's before we next delivered, hoping her connection would keep us on tap. I needed to refocus on the business. The idea that Tony Wehrmann would enact some sort of revenge for such a minor incident didn't even occur to me.

Melanie had different ideas, however. She came in the next morning and started to talk about how Wehrmann & Sons worked. More to the point, how they got around the law. George had boasted about many of the tricks. While I was no fan of liquor regulations, many of which were holdovers from Prohibition, I followed the law as best as possible and didn't like to hear about someone else breaking it. Especially my competitors. And since we distributed our own beer, Wehrmann & Sons was a competitor.

"Let's go see Sam," Melanie suggested, once she had loaded the pickup truck with kegs for deliveries.

"Who's Sam?"

"It's another place I worked. Not for long because I could never get him to put much on his taps beyond what he was told. Five minutes with him and you'll see why."

I nodded, wondering what she meant.

Jenna pulled up as we were leaving the brewery and I slowed, then stopped so our driver side doors were close. "How's Stan?" I asked.

"He's fine. How's Johnny?"

"You heard?"

"Word travels fast."

"He'll be okay. Needed a few stitches. They had to shave a little of his scalp; that bothered him more than anything. Melanie took him to the hospital."

Jenna leaned back so she could see Melanie. "Hello Melanie, how are you doing?"

"Well, I haven't gotten fired yet," Melanie replied.

"She's stellar," I said. "Loaded the truck without Johnny's help, *and* convinced him he didn't need to come in today. That was the more difficult task."

"Stan's the same, already wants to come back and work," Jenna replied. "I'm wondering if we'll need to open up a new wing for the non ambulatory."

"He's out of the hospital?"

"Yesterday. Felt funny rolling the wheelchair out again, this time with permission. He insisted on finding the same one, he's superstitious like that."

"The sign of a jock," I said. "So to what do we owe the pleasure of your visit?"

"I've decided you need help," Jenna said. "I plan to catch up on the books. I'd hoped to catch you before you left."

"You..." I started to say.

She held up her hand. "Look, without Stan you'll probably spend more time in the field and the paperwork needs to be done. The state needs their forms. And I know how much you hate paperwork."

"...don't have to," I finished.

Jenna looked at Melanie. "Has he gotten you on payroll?" Melanie glanced at me with an embarrassed look on her face. I shrugged. "You gave him the information he needed, right?" Melanie nodded. "I'm not surprised," Jenna said. "You two go do your deliveries and I'll get Mel set up. Is it okay if I call you Mel?"

"Sure."

"Good. When you come back, I'll have a few things for you to sign."

"Sorry," I said to Jenna.

"Oh, don't worry. When you decided to take over this company, I told Stan that you'd need office help. He and Nate hated it and you're no different. You're all much better in the field. You need someone to run the back room."

"Putting me in the same camp as those two is an undeserved compliment," I said.

"You're not as outgoing, but you are a people person just the same," Jenna replied.

"Melanie's information is in the middle drawer of my desk. The paperwork for the state and federal is in the second drawer on the left. I have fallen a little behind but we have a week before reports are due."

"I've taken some time off from work and Stan will be fine. I cleaned out one of the old freezers he used for home brewing, and bought a wholesale order of frozen dinners for him." My mouth dropped open. Jenna was a natural foods demon. "Just kidding," she continued. "But he'll be fine."

"I feel very confident leaving the fate of Callahans in your hands," I said. "Now Sarah and I can take that vacation." I smiled and pulled away.

Nate and Jenna, now there was a love story. Hard to believe given how well suited she and Stan were for each other, but there had been a time.

Nate had always been a popular guy, and had attracted women without even trying. They fluttered to him like moths to a flame, where, not surprisingly, they were burned. They never were the right type. Not strong and independent, like Jenna. When Nate met her, Sarah and I thought she was the one.

But something had happened and Jenna moved to the west coast. More than once Nate told me she was the only woman he ever loved. Jenna returned to visit her family occasionally and I once saw the powerful undercurrent that ran between them, one that made me believe him. Then she met Stan and before you knew it, the two of them were getting married. I didn't know much more than that.

We had thought it was a mistake at first, a rebound for her and a lucky shot for Stan. But Nate said otherwise. He told me that they were meant for each other. That he had trouble loving anyone and it had never come more clear than when he'd let her move to California. It had torn his heart out, he said, and he'd let it happen. He was entirely focused on building a career. It had been money over love, he said, as if knowing that the opportunity he'd had was a once in a lifetime shot.

I didn't believe him at the time. But when he was diagnosed with cancer, I did. He dealt with it well, saying Stan was the one for her. I often wondered if his loyalty to his friend had outbid his feelings for Jenna, and if his honor was what prevented him from love. Stan idolized Nate. He threw himself into this new project, and Nate brought them both on board. Yet I still sensed that undercurrent of feeling in Jenna, even after Nate's death. It was as if something that was meant to happen hadn't, and everyone had learned to live out what did happen as best as they could. It was as if Jenna and Stan's intensity was partly built on the emotions that had existed before. Given his death, things had turned out as well as could be expected, lending my brother a presence beyond his physical being.

"Turn here, left."

Melanie's direction pulled my wandering thoughts back to our job. I looked back into the truck. "Still one keg."

"I want to show you something," she said.

I followed her directions to the north side of town, where a bar I'd heard had a good tap selection was located. Sam's was located on a corner, and displayed several neon beer signs—micros as opposed to neons from the penguin pushers.

We pulled into a spot on the street. Several people sat eating a late lunch at tables inside. A couple sat quietly at the bar to the left of the dining area. The lights were dim. No one was behind the bar. We sat and waited. Melanie pointed out the knobs; they were all Wehrmann's.

"You speak like a distributor," I said after she'd pointed this out.

"What do you mean?" she asked, sounding offended.

"It reminds me of the first time I went to a good beer bar with Nate. By then I was a connoisseur. And he'd had the brewery for two years.

"We sit down," I continued, "and he reels off the distributors for each brand on tap. There were more back then."

"Your point?"

"As a connoisseur, I saw the beers. Nate saw who distributed them. I told him this. I also told him what was missing from the lineup, a Belgian style beer."

"There's a lesson in here," Melanie replied, softening. "I hear it coming."

I smiled. "You know me."

"You were a great teacher," she said. "You would tell a story to captivate us, then drop the lesson in there."

"Thank you." I was glad it was dark so she couldn't see me blush. "If it was just teaching that I'd had to do, I probably would have stayed out of trouble."

"So the lesson is we should see the beer—the style, not the distributor. If we can fill a gap we're helping the bar owner round out his offerings."

"You always caught on quickly," I replied.

"This guy's missing a good stout," Melanie offered.

"Good call."

"Now I'm going to give *you* a lesson," she countered.

I looked around and asked, as if on cue, "Where is the bar owner?"

"Sam's cooking," Melanie said. "He runs this place alone except at night."

"Not exactly the service you'd expect from a bar," I said, then added, "How does he keep the place going?"

"It's not always about that," Melanie replied. "Sam's customers are used to this."

"I guess it *is* my turn to learn something," I replied.

"We're just starting." Melanie smiled, then got off her bar stool. "I'll get him." She walked to the juke box, fed it a dollar and hit some buttons. As she returned to her seat, *Time is on My Side* began to play. Moments later the door to the kitchen cracked open and a voice called, "I'll be right there!" A head appeared. "Hi, Mel! Help yourself, almost finished with this order."

"We can wait!" Melanie called back.

I smiled. "You know your bars."

"George took me to all of them." Her mood turned.

"It's okay for you to do this? It must bring back memories you'd rather forget."

"I'd do well to face them," she said. "And better to do it with someone, as part of a job. I actually like a lot of these places. Small businesses trying to make a living."

It was another five minutes before Sam appeared, to serve two tables their meals. Melanie had already gone behind the bar and served us both a beer, me an IPA and herself a brown ale. We exchanged tastes. Mine was a west coast beer from Mandible Brewing, and while it was nice and hoppy, it could have been fresher. Melanie's beer was spot on.

"Not as fresh as it could be," she commented, confirming my observation.

"You don't buy your French bread from France," I said, quoting Mo.

"I love Mo," Melanie said.

"He has an ability to distill concepts."

Finally, Sam appeared at the bar. He apologized for the delay.

"Sam, this is Ed Callahan, of Callahans Brewery."

Sam reached out his hand. "Nice to meet you." He turned to Melanie. "So, how have you been? I haven't seen you in a while."

"I'm well," she said. "Working for Callahans now, while I finish school. I wanted to talk to you about your beer selection." Sam glanced quickly—almost nervously—at the knobs as Melanie continued. "Customers seemed to like it."

Sam's eyes were caught by movement at one of the tables he was serving. "I gotta get that, I'll be right back." He turned to go and I quickly pulled a twenty out of my wallet. "That one's on me," he said. "Good to see you, Mel."

We waited another ten minutes while we sipped our beers. Another group of people entered the bar and sat at one of the tables. Sam waited on them and the people at the end of the bar, a young couple must have been on their first date because the guy ran through every topic from sports to politics to his feelings on abortion while the woman quietly listened. I couldn't see that date going anywhere. We left.

Melanie was silent for a while. Then, suddenly, she burst out "He has fifteen knobs and he's afraid to give us one!"

"Why do you think that is?" I asked.

"He owes them! I wonder what they're giving him, neons, vacation tickets, or just keg discounts. Maybe they've got something else going on, something new. Maybe they're threatening to take away the discounts."

I was more sanguine, simply saying, "Maybe we need to get some people in there asking for our beer."

Melanie's head turned sharply and she stared at me. For a moment I thought she was going to accuse me of abandoning the fight, like I'd done at the university. But she said nothing, except, "It's just unfair."

As I turned onto the main thoroughfare toward the brewery, I spotted that lone full keg of beer, surrounded by empties. "I tell you what," I said, extending my hand. "I'll bet you a case I'll have our beer on at Sam's within a month." It was something Nate and I had always done, make bets after the inevitable disagreements between brothers.

"Done."

9

We returned to the brewery. Jenna's car was gone, replaced by Mo's. The door was open again, swinging on its hinges as if we ran the business out of an abandoned building. With colder weather approaching, I knew I had to get that fixed.

I backed the truck up to the loading dock and headed inside while Melanie waited. I stopped to fiddle with the door knob for a moment, then left it for someone more capable.

Stepping into the building in the afternoon always reminded me of Nate. He had remodeled the brewery to show its best side as you entered, blasting through brick to install giant windows high on the opposite wall. On sunny days like today, it reminded me of a magnificent old church, with the light playing on the wood rafters and brightening the interior. A huge skylight topped a roof that was inclined enough to force most of the winter snow off.

Callahans build out was Nate's dream. I thought the window project was too costly, but he'd pressed ahead with his vision. There was still some touch up work to be done—the dormer leaked from ice buildup, but the vision was impressive. The long term goal, of course, was to make it people friendly if and when regulations ever changed to allow us to serve at our place of business. That was another change Nate had gambled on.

I walked through the brewing area and opened the loading dock door. Tossing Melanie the pickup keys, I left her to unload the "needies," which was what empties were called once they passed through the loading dock into the brewery. I noticed Johnny's pack and heard noise behind the kettles, where the keg cleaner/filler was located. Johnny's bicycle leaned against Johnson. Johnny had decided to come in anyway, I thought. He'd probably say it was only a flesh wound.

Mo was at his desk in the office, sitting behind a beer and four tasting glasses. On his desk was a paper weight that read GM, which he told everyone, "stands for 'Good Morning.'" Johnny said the desk sign should read PM given Mo's late working hours.

A small stack of papers lay on my desk, neatly lined up and with tabs noting where I should sign. Envelopes were clipped to each form. A note on the top explained what was to be done with each one and when. Jenna would bring some welcome organization to the paperwork.

"You and Johnny get those kegs filled?" I asked. "The Lodge called to say they ran out of Copper."

"Haven't done that yet," Mo replied, carefully pouring the beer into the glasses.

"What am I paying you for?" I joked.

"You pay peanuts, you get monkeys," Mo replied, setting down the empty bottle.

I chuckled. "Where'd you end up last night?" After we had dropped Johnny's car off at his apartment, Mo said he wanted to go out. I had been too tired.

"The Spittoon. Had a couple of Scotches with my beer."

"That's why it smells like cigars in here." I wrinkled my nose.

"Had to have my vegetables, too," Mo replied. The Spittoon was one of the only places in the state where smoking was allowed, an exemption having been grandfathered in because they sold so much tobacco when the anti-smoking laws began to be enacted. While I welcomed a smoke free environment, a lot of bar owners felt that the law hurt their businesses. That, combined with the lower blood alcohol content levels for DWI laws, had been a one-two punch that put a few places out of business. The Spittoon had done better. A lot of people still wanted to smoke inside and many of them went there and experienced the better beer selection. As Mo said, "They go in smokin' and come out drinkin' our beer!"

"We still on there?" I asked.

Mo gave me a thumbs up sign. "Half my liver resides in that place."

Mo was one of the few investors that actually got a paycheck. He had been a friend of Nate's in college, but instead of joining the corporate world when he graduated he'd traveled. "Dodging work and working on his dodge," Nate used to say about his friend and our head brewer. He'd decided to stay abroad, teaching in American schools and saving money. Mo had always claimed that Nate was going to do something big one day and he wanted to be a part of it. He turned out to be right, became an investor and made himself essential by studying at Weihenstephan, a prestigious brewing school in Germany. More than just a friend, he was an honest, hardworking employee who Nate couldn't say enough about. I'd come to rely on my brother's opinions about people and trusted Mo completely.

Mo also provided a window into my brother's life. They were complete opposites in personality, but having spent so much time together, Mo brought along stories of Nate's college exploits, which he was always willing to share. Since I hadn't seen Nate a lot during those years, I enjoyed hearing the stories.

One of my favorites was the time that they were walking home after a night out, in the middle of winter. They'd had a little too much beer and about one hundred yards from their apartment, Nate had collapsed in a snow bank. Mo had tried to get him to get up and move and my brother refused, saying he wasn't going a step farther without a beer. Mo told him there was one in the fridge back at the apartment but Nate again said no, that he wanted the beer right here. Mo claimed Nate would have frozen to death if he'd left him there. Or perhaps he was unsure of whether he'd be able to get back to him with the beer. At any case he refused to leave him and Nate finally got back up and trudged home, berating his friend the entire way for not bringing him a beer. When they reached the apartment, Nate fell to the floor and slept there all night. Mo maintained that the incident pushed my brother to open a brewery, so he'd never have to walk that far again for a beer.

"Where's Johnny?" Mo asked, pointing to the half-filled glasses in front of him.

I picked one up. "He's cleaning needies. Thought you'd seen him."

"I've been hiding in here."

Melanie entered. "Hey beautiful," Mo said. "You're back early."

"She's efficient," I said. "We even stopped at a new place to try to cement a knob."

"Where?" Mo asked.

"Sam's," Melanie said.

"Ooo..." Mo said. "That would be a coup."

"Ed says he's going to sell them within a month," Melanie replied.

Mo looked at me, surprised.

"I bet her," I said. "Someone has to step into Stan's shoes while Mel learns the ropes."

"You're acting more like your brother each day," Mo observed. "He'd be proud."

The door opened again and Johnny entered. A white bandage covered his stitches.

"Hey J, you pop too many steroids yesterday?" Mo said.

"No steroids," Johnny replied, flexing his arms.

"You were *mucho* aggressive last night," Mo continued. Johnny shrugged. "I tell you—you left that group of penguins with their lips rattlin'. They didn't know what hit 'em."

Melanie neared Johnny and looked closely at the bandage. "Looks clean," she said.

"It won't get in the way of what I gotta do today," Johnny said.

"I thought I told you to take a day off," I said.

"Too much to do," Johnny replied. "I thought with Stan gone I'd get a breather, but you guys sell Mo's shit like it's actually good. You're making my job harder than it should be." His lopsided grin was more noticeable because the right side of his mouth seemed to droop under the bandage. He caught sight of the glasses on Mo's desk. "Don't tell me we have to try another one of your brain farts."

"You don't have to try nothin', sport," Mo shot back. "But some day, your palate may wake up and you'll realize that fast food isn't all there is to life."

I loved this office banter, so different from what went on at the university, where professors were isolated in offices and rarely had daily contact with each other. There had been meetings but the repartee was more ethereal, almost as if once you reached that level of academia, you lost your grounding. Near the end of my time there, given my troubles, I had felt even more isolated. At Callahans, the one-upmanship also allowed people to release any tension that might build up from daily chores. I often wondered if that kind of communication would have prevented the blowout

I'd had with the university's department chair. Sarah said yes, but I thought the issues sunk deeper.

Johnny picked up one of the glasses and sniffed it. "Smells like charcoal."

"Good," Mo said. "You're learning."

"Did you notice that street light?" Johnny asked me.

"Which one?"

"The one on the corner. Somebody screwed with it."

"What do you mean?"

"I rode my bike in this morning and saw the cover was off at the bottom of the pole."

"Who would want to do that?" I asked.

"No reason that I can see," Johnny replied. "Unless you wanted to kill the light."

"Is it working?" I asked. I looked at Mo, who did the late shift.

"Far as I remember, it was," he said. "I'll check it this evening."

10

The next afternoon I decided to return to Sam's. I wanted to cement a knob and if there was one thing I had learned from Nate, it was the necessity for persistence. So many of the trophies he'd piled up had come from to his determination to push himself, never give up. That determination had made him a top salesman several times, before he decided to build the brewery. I wasn't the greatest salesman, but everyone had to pitch in if Callahans was to be successful. Besides, I had a bet to win with Melanie.

She dropped me off and took over the rest of the route, promising to return when I was ready to leave. Driving each other home was as much standard procedure as knowing the roads least likely to harbor police, both good ways to avoid a Diwi. Nate usually got one of the bartenders—or a woman he'd enamored—to give him a ride, but everyone in the company knew playing taxi was part of the job. It didn't matter what time it was; a call meant you needed a ride.

Sam's seemed smaller than I remembered, a narrow room only thirty yards long. In the back left ran a bar with a dozen stools. A dining area partially blocked by a makeshift wall and rest rooms blossomed to the right. Toward the rear a doorway led into the kitchen. The door had been removed, allowing the cook to see and hear the barroom while working.

The walls were decorated with a scattered mishmash of point of sale materials—posters celebrating Oktoberfests, special brewery offerings, and a spot for photos of customers enjoying one past event or another. With the neons lining the upper halves of the front windows, the lower halves held the more transient events posters.

The wall beyond the bar had a Fans of Sam's Club, names glued to a board that appeared to have been abandoned. Sam's was too small for a massive crowd, but big enough to host a regular, loyal following.

I ordered a Barrels Pilsner, interested to know how our closest competitor was doing. The beer seemed cleaner than I remembered, a good sign, but still not as daring a product as Mo brewed. It was a style "steeped in mediocrity" Mo always said.

There was good reason for this. As a beer style, pilsner was what the major breweries offered. So when small breweries started brewing the style, they used it as a crossover, a beer for people new to the scene and not wanting too much flavor. Thus pilsner had lagged behind other more daring styles in the microbrewery explosion. That Barrels was brewing it without pushing the flavor envelope was a good thing, according to Mo. A cautious competitor made us look better.

While I sipped the Pilsner, I looked around. I'd heard Sam had a steady retinue of customers who came and went, often for just a quick beer and a chat. At lunch and dinner time, other regulars came in for a meal. On the slow days, like today, he worked the place alone. I was reminded of England, where pubs were a greater part of the community fabric. Sarah and I had traveled there several times, visiting relatives north of London, and we had spent a lot of our time dining and drinking in the pubs. While different in decoration, especially the tvs, Sam's was really an English pub, the kind of place where a person could spend some time. Even me, if Sam put one of our beers on tap.

"I like the place," I said, catching the owner in one of his brief lunch crowd appearances behind the bar.

"Thanks," Sam replied. "The landlord hasn't done much upkeep, but we manage."

"The bar has character." I meant it. Character was what so many microbrewery bars boasted. They weren't fashioned from a market study and an accountant's pen, instead used the space allotted them, previously something entirely different. From the rearranged two family houses of Seattle to the open space warehouses of New York City, these bars embodied the creativity of the industry. Nate had called the microbrewery bars the "mitochondria of the movement," each place offering its customers a rich variety of the beverage that had ignited their passion. Bars were the little powerhouses that drove so many small, independent breweries to success.

Sam was an enigma. Like a lot of bar owners, he was independent, highly opinionated, and friendly. Independent mindedness was one of the traits I liked most about bar owners in our country. Unlike Europe, where so many of bars were owned by the breweries that limited their offerings, U.S. bar owners bought the products they wanted. This independence had been essential for the spread of microbrewery beers like ours.

Despite his independent spirit, though, I sensed something else at work in Sam. I got an inkling of what that was indirectly. And it confirmed what Melanie had maintained, that he was afraid of something.

My insight came with the mid-afternoon slowdown in customers. Sam had finished in the kitchen and was cleaning up the bar area. I had nursed the Pilsner and when he stayed I ordered another beer, a dunkel. It was also mediocre, and as it warmed, the house flavor Mo talked about emerged.

While he filled me a second pint, Sam glanced at the only other two people in the bar, a couple who sat close together whispering to each other. "How are the lovebirds today?" he called. They giggled. Sam turned to me. "Nice to be young," he said.

I nodded. "Lends a whole new perspective to life."

"Yeah," Sam said. "This beer is on me."

I scanned the tap handles and said, "A stout would make a good addition to your lineup."

Sam looked up quickly, surprised. Or was it fear? I wasn't sure.

"Just a thought," I added. "You could use a good stout."

Sam pointed to the tap of Guinness. "That seems to work."

"Something local," I replied. Guinness Stout was a standard in most bars, and while many owners thought it covered the dark end of the spectrum, good bars went beyond it.

"I couldn't take Guinness off," Sam said. "I'd piss off too many customers."

"We have a good stout," I said. "Have you ever tasted Callahans stout? It's called Black Pudding."

A man entered, his hello interrupting our conversation. He was dressed in jeans and a military shirt. It was the new military, revealing wars being fought in deserts instead of jungles. Sam got him a bottle of Budweiser, no glass.

"How you doing, Len?"

"Fine, now," Len replied, picking up the bottle and drinking half of it. "The day has began."

I resisted the temptation to correct his grammar, remembering that I was no longer at the university. Ever the teacher, however, I couldn't resist pushing the beer. "Ever try that Pilsner?" I asked, pointing to the Barrels knob.

He looked at me for a long moment, then shook his head. "Bud does the job. And it's an American beer."

"Actually, the big guys are owned by international money. If you want a strictly American beer, you'll have to step up to the microbrewed level."

"They still got a plant in St. Louis," Len replied, "and that's good enough for me." He finished the bottle and signaled for another.

Sam pulled another bottle of Budweiser out of the cooler and de-capped it. He slid it toward Len, then poured a taste of Barrels Pilsner and put it in front of him. "Try it again," he said. "It's gotten better."

Len picked it up and drank it. Then nodded. "Not bad."

"Let me know when you want one," Sam said, winking at me.

I had to admire him. This was how customers were brought into the fold, a taste and no pressure. Some would never change, but others would come around. "I can get you something more flavorful than Guinness," I said, deciding to continue the conversation. "At a competitive price."

Sam was washing bar glasses and his movements suddenly seemed to grow more erratic, less logical. He began to put clean glasses on the bar top. Then he'd take them off the bar top and put them behind the bar, on the shelves. There was definitely something wrong, I thought. Finally, he looked up and said, "Len, this is Ed Callahan. Owns a brewery."

"That's why you're trying to get me to drink that micro stuff," Len replied.

I nodded, but said nothing.

"You with the Wehrmanns?"

"No," I replied. "You know them?"

"I know Tony. I was with him in Iraq." He pronounced it "Eye-rack." At first it was just small talk, where he'd been stationed, that he'd been with the first troops in and the stunned silence of most of the people he'd encountered. But by his third bottle of beer he steered the conversation back to Tony Wehrmann.

"Now *he* was crazy," Len said, the alcohol loosening his tongue. "I could see it in his eyes, every time we went out. He always talked about how jealous he was of the privates."

"The privates?" I asked.

"Private contractors. Guys that got started in the military and were hired by a private company. They were all over the place. Had no rules."

I nodded, ready to let the whole conversation drop, but Len kept talking. "He looked for reasons to shoot at somebody. He was mean."

"What do you mean?" I asked. Sam continued to wash glasses behind the bar.

"I remember being with him in a Humvee once when we came up on this Haji whose car broke down on a bridge. He hit the horn and waved and the guy waved out his window. His hood was up. 'You gotta get off the fucking bridge!' he yelled, and the guy waved and yelled something. His car was broke down."

Out of the corner of my eye I could see Sam, washing glasses a little more vigorously. "Wehrmann says "Fuck 'em!" and rams the car. Pushes it right off the bridge, driver and all."

I hid my emotions and asked, "What happened?"

"They sent him home before he killed someone. Not good for the business."

"I meant what happened to the Iraqi," I replied, still not able to react.

"Who knows?"

I left Sam's shortly after that, promising to stop back with samples of our stout. When Melanie arrived, I asked, "What do you know about Tony Wehrmann?"

"I heard he was in the military," she replied, confirming the bar regular's claim. "Then got discharged. His father gave him a job in the company."

We rode in silence for a while. Then Melanie turned to me, excited. "I almost forgot to mention. Johnny says it's a front blinker."

"What?" I asked, a little slowed by the beer.

"That light you picked up at the accident. It's a front blinker. Someone pushed Stan off the road."

I finally understood what she was talking about, but only nodded.

"They'll all be in the yard."

"What?"

"The delivery trucks. They'll all be in the yard now. We can go check them out."

"They'll have cameras."

"No cameras," she says. "And there's a door to the fence gate that's easy to pick."

Given what I'd just heard at the bar, it seemed that now was the time to act.

11

The darkness overwhelmed me. Complete darkness.

I had gotten a call from Melanie. She needed help and she didn't say why. I drove to her parents' home outside the city. It was pitch black. I felt surrounded by a dull, nameless dread. Melanie got into the back seat of the car. I sensed that someone was after her. She didn't speak. She didn't have to.

As we drove away from her house, two thin columns of smoke rose out of the furnace chimney. Each column changed from an amorphous mass into a human-like shape. "My parents," Melanie said quietly. I didn't understand, didn't reply.

An elementary school parking lot appeared ahead, one lone street light in its middle. I pulled into the lot and drove across the carefully painted lines, parking in the middle of the open space. A pickup cruised past, its headlights off. It circled us, a shark assessing its prey. A man peered out of the window. The pickup stopped and the man got out. He was wearing a camouflage uniform and carrying a double-barrel shotgun. He asked if Melanie was with me. I said nothing. She sat waiting, mute. But he wasn't leaving.

Melanie said something. She got out of the car and walked toward the shadows of the elementary school building. Just before she disappeared I noticed that she wore a heavy coat that concealed all but her bare legs. She wore no shoes.

The man followed. It was Tony Wehrmann. A flash of fear struck me. That didn't seem right. The fear grew into urgency, a need to act. He disappeared into the shadows. I heard a scream.

I grabbed my phone to call the police. I tried to turn it on as a second scream followed, then a third. I fumbled with the phone, but it wouldn't turn on.

A shadow ran across the dark, open space behind the building. Another shadow followed, this one a black outline with a shotgun raised above its head. The shotgun rose and fell.

I leapt out of the car and ran toward the two figures. It was too dark to see, but I heard the screams again. They were calling my name. The voice sounded familiar.

"Ed!... Ed!"

I awoke, tense, sleep erased from my mind.

"What was it?" Sarah asked. She lay next to me on the bed, propped up on one elbow. "You were panting and mumbling, almost crying."

"Water," I replied.

She got up and disappeared into the bathroom. I glanced at the clock. It was 2:30 in the morning.

When Sarah returned I told her the dream. Then started to fill her in on what had happened since Stan's accident.

"I'm surprised by that," she said when I got to the bar incident.

"Really?" I replied. "You know Johnny."

"Not that it had happened, but that it's the first time you've mentioned it."

"You've...we've both been busy." There were often periods when Sarah and I rarely crossed paths until night, settling a kiss on a sleeping companion, missing our morning coffee together. This was one of those times. I had spent longer hours than usual at work and Sarah had been preparing her students for mid-term exams.

"We always manage to speak about the bigger things, and this is big," she said. "Especially given your initial suspicions about Stan's accident."

"That didn't turn out to be anything we could nail down," I replied. "We even checked out the trucks and none of them had any turn lights missing."

"Who?"

"Who what?"

"Who checked out the trucks?"

"Melanie and I."

"You didn't tell me about that either."

I could sense annoyance by the quietness in her response. "You were asleep when I got home," I said.

"You usually call to say when you're working late."

I changed the subject. "I can't figure out the dream. To me it seems based on a fear I have for Melanie, combined with fatherly feelings. She's young, involved in something dangerous, and I'm unable to help. Or may even be the cause of the danger."

"You've had similar dreams."

"When?" I asked, glad she decided to overlook the communication issue.

"When you were fighting your windmill struggle with the university. Remember? Except I was the little girl you couldn't rescue." She snuggled up close and wrapped her arms around me.

"And in the end you rescued me." I kissed her.

"Oh that reminds me. Randy Brinkworth called. That lawyer from the university."

Mention of Brinkworth brought back a tumult of memories. I often thought how funny it was that things had worked out the way they had, how fate dealt a stronger hand than any we could conjure. The research I had been conducting to link the high rate of cancer in my childhood neighborhood with a nearby industrial chemical plant had finally borne fruit; there was a provable connection between the two. This was not big news in the environmental community—dozens of these sites had been revealed around the country. But my research had become politically charged because Arnold Guthman, the plant's owner and the person after whom it was named, was a wealthy patron of the university. Documents I'd dug up—in what was as much a sleuthing operation as a piece of scientific research—

revealed that he had hired an unlicensed trash disposal company to dispose of large amounts of waste. And Arnold Guthman was about to have the university's new chemistry building he had endowed named after him.

Moreover, it would be hard to sweep this one under the rug, because my friend John Biers was the local newspaper's city editor at the time, and had been following my work closely. He planned to run a larger story that would prove embarrassing to all involved. The university administration—the Chemistry Department chair to be exact—had asked me to hold off on the story. The reasoning was that at a later date this would blow over. The scandal behind the name would be less harmful after the building had been christened. Especially once the students from my human ecology course had graduated, or left for the summer. Brinkworth came in as the lawyer for the state's environmental regulatory outfit.

I had decided to be interviewed for the story. It turned out to be fortunate that I had somewhere to go, a new project that meant something more than a professorship with an angry leadership. I had the brewery.

"So did you find anything out at the yard, you and your new girlfriend?" Sarah asked, interrupting my thoughts.

"We were too busy having wild sex on top of one of the vans," I replied.

"Right."

"I'm not kidding. I'm confessing."

"I know you better than that," Sarah said. "She would have had to make the first move."

"You don't think she wants me? I'm not attractive anymore?"

Sarah rolled on her side to face me. "Of course you are, honey."

"If you'd been there I would have pinned you up against one of those trucks and had you right there. One kiss and you'd have been mine."

Sarah giggled. "How about one of those kisses right now?"

I took her hand and kissed it, then started to work my way up her arm, kissing her slowly as she murmured in delight. Our mouths found each other, then our bodies. It had been a while since we'd made love and it brought us closer, our bodies enmeshed, our breathing in unison again.

Suddenly Sarah pulled away and rolled onto her back. "Let's take a look at what you have."

"Detective time? It's three in the morning!"

"You're not going to pull one of those, 'I've had my sex, goodnight' routines, are you?" She laughed and continued. "Besides, I'm bored at work. Same old routine, except for the kids. But even some of them start to blend into stereotypes. Hard-working, lazy, angry, happy, sloppy, obsessive-compulsive, easily distracted."

"There's not much to say," I replied.

"When did the suspicions start?"

"When Stan went off the road. He can't remember how that happened."

"So Stan goes off the road on a corner known for accidents. You stop to see whether there is anything suspicious, and find a stray cover from a turn signal light. Did you have that checked out?"

"I asked Brindisi, the officer who arrived at the accident scene."

"What did he say?"

"Looked at me like I was from another planet."

"And Johnny doesn't know anything about it?"

I shook my head.

"What's next?" Sarah asked.

"The door was open at the brewery office the next morning."

"What's so significant about that?"

"It's usually locked. Turns out that Stan was inside. Gave us a bit of a scare."

"Let's discard that."

"Next day the outside door is wide open."

"That door has been broken forever. It could have blown open with a strong gust of wind."

"Then there's the cut wires on the…no, wait, I forgot to mention that Melanie knows the Wehrmanns. She says they're bad news."

"You're clogging up the logic path with suppositions," Sarah said. "Let's follow the path of facts and see if it leads anywhere. What about the wires?"

"The wires on the street lamp outside the brewery were cut."

"That's strange. Who could have done that?"

"Not sure. But it doesn't seem like just anyone."

"Why not?"

"Because..."

"And why would someone cut wires?" Sarah interrupted. "It seems like too much work for a vandal when they could just throw a rock at the light."

To tell the truth, I had forgotten about the street light with everything else going on. I made a mental note to report it to our local precinct. "I don't know what that was about," I said. "I asked Johnny to take a closer look and let me know."

"What about the fight?"

"A misogynist got his comeuppance," I replied.

"What happened?"

"Tony Wehrmann—he's the crazy brother, supposedly—insulted Melanie and Johnny came up out of his chair and knocked him on his ass. Like he was back on the football field."

"Then what happened?"

"The cops stopped anything from happening further. It was at Benson's, a cop bar, and they were all at the place. That's also where I saw Brindisi again and asked him about the piece of signal light."

"What did he say?"

"He pooh-poohed my suspicions. I think he has bigger fish to fry."

"So you gave this crazy guy a reason for future action," Sarah said.

"Oh, and somehow Johnny got cut, a nice gash that took three stitches."

"Somehow?"

"He says he didn't see anything, just felt the blood running down his cheek. Melanie noticed it and hustled him out of the bar to the hospital while everyone else was still milling around."

"Do you think it was a knife?"

"Wouldn't surprise me. But Wehrmann would have had to have had it in his hand because Johnny's hit was fast. There would have been no time for him to pull anything out of his pocket."

"So that's all you got?" Sarah asked.

"I know it's not enough to inspire one of your students to write a mystery, but it's the truth."

"Truth can be boring." Then, as if to soften her response, Sarah added, "But it could be something."

"Really?" I asked.

"Less than fifty percent. But keep me informed."

12

That morning Jenna's car was outside the brewery, reminding me that I hadn't mailed the forms she'd finished. The brewery door had a large, laminated poster taped to it with my cell number on it, for deliveries. Johnny had promised to do that after we missed a morning yeast shipment during the uproar over Stan's accident. The door felt secure so he must have fixed that, too. It was good having a handy man around.

Jenna sat at my desk. The books—or what I had inherited from Nate and called the books—were scattered across the top of my desk.

"How's Stan?" I asked.

"Fine, except he wants to come back to work."

"And Junior?"

Jenna smiled. "He's great. Talks about going to school all the time. You'd think he didn't want to be home with mom." She held up a sheaf of papers. "Looks like I caught this just in time. Brew quantities are due at the end of the month. We miss one of these and we'll start getting registered letters."

I winced in embarrassment. "I was going to talk to you about that."

"Did you mail those letters?"

"Going to do that today."

"How about payroll?"

"I have a handle on it. In fact, I have to cut a check for Stan." Nate had prided himself in paying everyone on time, with checks that didn't bounce.

"He doesn't want it."

"That's ridiculous. It isn't his fault that he's out of work."

"I know, but we're thinking of the company. And a few things need fixing around here. I have a salary so we'll do fine."

"We can afford it. Why not buy something for yourselves?"

"I noted it in here. Just keep track of how much it is and consider it equity," Jenna replied, indicating that the decision had been made. "I'd be happy to do payroll," she added.

I shrugged. "It's all in there. You're welcome to it."

"Data backed up?"

I winced again.

"I hope you don't think I'm being too nosy."

"Not at all. I appreciate the help. I can get to some other things that need to be done. Johnny's been bugging me about sealing the skylight before winter. Last year there was some leakage." In fact, I would be happy to give up the monthly kabuki dance to balance the books. From the beginning, paying bills, which Nate hadn't spoken much about, was a chore. It always seemed that one last check would arrive to cover them. We were like a lot of small businesses in America, I imagined. I walked around my desk.

"Don't mess up my piles," Jenna said quickly. "They're organized. Like yesterday, all you have to do is sign and seal. And mail,"she added.

"I just need the key to open the bay door, for keg deliveries. Mel will be here soon."

While I was searching for the key, Mo entered. He was wearing shorts, a tee shirt and sandals, despite the cooler weather. He wore shorts throughout year, but changed to hiking boots in winter unless he was brewing. Mo was skinny for his age, as if his metabolism had never slowed down. And he ate constantly, whatever he wanted. Nate used to say he burned off the calories with his creativity gene. The rest of us were just envious.

Surprised to see our brewer before noon, I was about to say something when Johnny entered. He had his backpack slung over his shoulder, hadn't yet changed into his keg monkey outfit. He looked at Mo. "What are you doing here? Come up with some new idea for a fruit beer to clog up the mash tun?"

"Ah, the Neanderthal himself," Mo replied. He walked to the small office refrigerator and pulled it open. "What will it be today, Johnny, another Copper?"

"A solid beer," Johnny retorted. "Recipe was the Man's and you're jealous." Nate had designed the beer before Mo had come on board. Mo had tinkered with it, but the beer was seen as Nate's baby.

A bottle flew across the room and Johnny moved quickly.

"Nice catch," Mo said. "Anyone else?" Jenna and I shook our heads.

"When you gonna cut that hair?" Johnny asked Mo. "It's a mess."

"When you pull your pants up," Mo replied.

The two were from different generations, but even without Stan here to run interference they worked like a team. Mo made the beer and knew every facet of brewing and recipe formulation, and Johnny was a mechanical whiz, able to repair and improve upon the equipment Mo needed to produce his magic. Like so many small breweries, we had cobbled together a brewhouse from new and used equipment. Even the new equipment had faults given the youth of the small brewery industry. My team shared cleanup, the great unwanted task in brewing because it was so constant and so necessary.

Melanie entered. She was wearing a light beige jacket over her orange shirt and jeans.

"Hello Melanie," Jenna said. "How are things going?"

"Hi," Melanie replied. "Great! I *love* selling beer!"

Johnny watched her take off the jacket and walked over to her. "I'll take that." He took the jacket and walked to the small closet to hang it up.

"You don't have to do that," Melanie said.

"Ooooo…" Mo said. "From rude boy to boy wonder in seconds."

"Someone's got to step up around here," Johnny replied, then looked at me. "To follow in Ed's footsteps."

"Nice recovery," I said.

"Nice for Johnny," Mo added. "He's in the ten second program. It takes him ten seconds to think of a comeback. By then it's usually too late."

"The problem with you," Johnny shot back, "is you've reached the point where the number of beers you've drunk is greater than your remaining brain cells. Impressive drinking, but not a good long term strategy." He turned to Melanie. "Unfortunately, I don't see many years left for your friend."

"Beers and brain cells, the numbers still outmatch yours in both categories," Mo replied.

Melanie's smile remained frozen on her face and I wondered if this was the first time she'd seen Mo and Johnny in their chronic battle of wits. Johnny finished his beer and put the bottle down on Mo's desk. "I got work to do."

"Average White Band. 1974. Before your time."

Melanie turned to go. "I'll help Johnny get the deliveries loaded in the pickup." Mo got up, too, and the three filed out of the office.

"So this is what you encounter every day?" Jenna asked, once everyone had left.

"Beer and banter. It keeps things lively around here."

"No wonder Stan wants to return. He'd banter his life away if I didn't have a list of things for him to do at home."

"It usually doesn't start until afternoon, when Mo gets in. He's in early today."

Jenna pointed to my desk and I sat down and began signing the forms. Once I'd finished, she made copies and sealed the letters in their envelopes.

"I'm going by the post office," she said. "Get me the two letters from yesterday and I'll drop them all off. Enjoy your day."

Once Jenna had left, I looked around. Mention of Stan's return, while not immediate, made me wonder how to fit another desk in the office. Everyone had a desk except Melanie, who was using Stan's. And what would I put on her desk sign? Years ago, Nate had bought carved wooden signs for each desk that best summed up his team's daily habits. Stan's sign read, *Beer, is there anything it can't do?* Johnny's read, *You can't drink all day if you don't start in the morning,* and Mo's read, *Beer is the reason I get up each afternoon.* I'd have to come up with something appropriate for Melanie.

Mo reappeared and sat at his desk, which was covered with recipe formulations and assorted beers from breweries around the country.

"To what do we owe this early morning honor?" I asked.

"We need to talk," he replied.

"About what?"

"Melanie told me."

"What did she tell you?"

"Ed, when something like this comes up, you need to let me know. I'm a shareholder."

"You mean my suspicions about the Wehrmanns?" Mo didn't reply. "What do you think I should do?"

"I think you should get the police involved."

I shook my head, remembering my conversation with Brindisi. And that I had his business card.

Johnny reentered the office. Followed by Melanie.

"Like I said, we need to talk," Mo repeated.

I looked at three grim faces, taken aback. Then suspicious that everything I said had been shared. I started slowly. "I … want you to know that whatever I've said until now has been an over-reaction. First Nate, then Stan…it's been a difficult time. So I apologize for my suspicions. Sarah, who has the best analytical mind I know, thinks there is nothing to all this. But she's keeping an open mind."

"What did I tell you!" Johnny said. "I went along with it because if it involves danger to Stan, I'm in. But I never believed it, even when you two ganged up on me." He looked at Mo and Melanie triumphantly, then added, "Mo thinks everything is a conspiracy."

"You're right, Johnny," Mo replied, making eyebrows raise. "Pardon me for thinking that the powerful would ever conspire to protect their interests. How stupid of me." That was more like the Mo I knew.

Melanie kept silent. I think she felt bad this had ever come up. Or maybe guilty for being part of it.

"I'm not writing anything off," I said. "I just know I've been a little jumpy lately, and need to think things through."

"Tell him," Mo said, looking at Johnny.

Johnny frowned, then said, "The cut wires. Whoever did it used a star wrench to get into the box."

"One that's not commonly available," Mo added.

"What would be the purpose?" I asked. "Besides to kill that light."

"It's not as if they cut the power to the brewery," Mo added.

"Darkness hides camera footage," Johnny said.

I sat down and wondered what Nate would do, which is what I did whenever something that seemed beyond my capabilities occurred. What would a brother with greater ambition and ability do? The three of them sat quietly, waiting. I knew they weren't short on opinions, especially Mo, but they knew enough to keep them to themselves for now. They would wait to see what Nate would say. He had conditioned them well.

Was I good enough to be in this position? It was a question I asked myself often.

I was about to speak when a loud crash sounded outside the office. Then a thump, like something hitting the floor.

Johnny was the first out the door. "Something fell through the skylight!"

We all crowded outside the office. In the middle of the brewery floor lay a crumpled human body, its head twisted oddly. Although I'd never seen a dead person before, I knew this was one. And recognized him. It was Randall Brinkworth.

13

"He smells like a brewery," Brindisi said, staring at the blanket-covered body. I looked up and saw that Brindisi was smiling at his own joke. He had been the first officer to arrive.

I looked up at the broken skylight, from where the body had fallen. "What was he doing on the roof?"

"That's what I was going to ask you. Do you know him?"

"I recognize him," Johnny said. "But he usually knocked on the door to get his beer."

"So he came here often?" Brindisi reflected, ignoring Johnny's black humor.

Johnny nodded. "And brought his growler to fill."

"What's a growler?"

"Half gallon container to carry beer." I pointed to a display across the room, where the pouring station was. "People can get draught beer to go."

"He didn't bring one, so he wasn't coming for beer," Brindisi observed. "Question is, what was he doing carrying a gun?"

"He called me yesterday," I said.

Brindisi looked up from his note taking. "What did he want?"

"Don't know, I wasn't home. He left a message to call him and that was about it. It just happened yesterday. I was too busy to get back to him."

"Wasn't home?" Brindisi asked.

"He left the message on my home phone."

"What did he say?" Brindisi started to work his tongue inside his mouth, as if he was trying to dislodge a piece of food from his molars. His cheek puffed out slightly as he kept his eyes on me.

"Nothing beyond to call him."

"How did you know him?"

"Through the university. Not *from* there, but when I worked there. He was a lawyer for the state environmental agency at the time."

"Is that all?"

"I saw him in court once, when I took my class there to observe a case involving the Sand Ridge landfill." A blank look came over Brindisi's face and I explained. "It was a while back. When the landfill was still operating."

"But you don't know what he wanted when he called you." I shook my head, and Brindisi added, "Seems coincidental."

"What do you mean?"

"He calls you. The next day he shows up dead." Brindisi nodded toward the blanketed figure on the floor. "Where you work."

"I agree. And wish I could help."

"What about the ladder?"

I looked at him. Then understood what he was asking. "The skylight was leaking and Johnny here was going to fix it."

"I just put the ladder there two days ago," Johnny added.

Brindisi nodded. "Okay. If you remember anything else, call me at this number." He handed me a business card. I noticed that it said Investigator, different than the one he'd given me at Benson's. I wondered if, like other city employees that were being downsized, he was doing double duty. "Can I get up on the roof?" he asked.

"Ladder's outside," Johnny said. "I gotta get up there and repair the hole so let me know when I can go up there."

Johnny left and at first Brindisi said nothing, just watched me, his tongue still working inside his mouth. Finally, he asked "Any other active businesses around here where someone might have seen him on the roof?"

I shook my head. "Maybe a passersby. This is a pretty dead area, we're the first to start a business here in decades."

"I'll see what I can from the roof." He turned away, then back. "What was it you were telling me when I saw you in Benson's?"

"That was about the accident my sales guy was in," I replied. "I thought at the time it looked suspicious. My guy's a good driver and doesn't drink while he's driving."

"Maybe we should go over that."

Johnny arrived and motioned toward the door. "Ladder's up."

Before Brindisi left he asked, "Tell me again where you were when you heard the body fall."

"In the office." I pointed. "We were all in there."

Brindisi and Johnny left and I looked around. A second officer was waiting for someone to transport the body, but other than that the area was empty. Once the police had arrived, my staff had returned to work. It wasn't callousness, just that we were always a few steps behind and standing around gawking wasn't going to help.

I wondered if there would be a problem with regulations regarding the sky light. It was one of the improvements Nate had put up quickly, hoping to get some natural light into the brewery. The work was shoddy, at least that's what Johnny had said. It needed repair. Whether it did or not, it obviously had weakened to the point where a body could break through. Looking up I could see it was just the glass and inner framing that had broken. The outside frame appeared solid. I made a mental note to check pricing for a new one, hoping Johnny would get the measurements while he was up there.

Melanie approached me. "O'Toole's called, said they needed another keg of Copper."

"We'd better get it there right away, or they'll put something else on tap. Johnny's up on the roof, I'll help you get the keg."

"I got it covered," Melanie replied. "I put it in with the orders, just need to load them into the pickup."

She held out her hand and I handed her the keys. "Thanks. You sure you don't need help?"

"Mo's already moving kegs to the loading dock. You got enough to deal with. By the way, I remember that guy. He's the one we watched in court, right?"

I nodded, then remembered that Melanie had been in my course at the time. "And he came around here now and then, to buy beer. He never said much, just got his beer and left." Melanie turned to go. "I'm going back to Sam's this evening, try to cement that knob," I said.

"That's your third visit."

"All I get is three strikes?"

"No such rule. You get as many strikes as it takes."

"You sound like Nate."

"How long is this gonna tie us up?" It was Mo, pushing the keg dolly.

"Everything all right?" I asked.

"Keg Day was supposed to be tomorrow. Will the dead lawyer force us to postpone?"

"I don't think so," I replied. "I'll ask the officer."

Suddenly Mo's face lit up. "I've got it!" I looked at him, surprised. "A name for the new beer." I looked at him, puzzled. "Dead Lawyer," he said. "It'll be a sellout."

"I like it," Melanie added before I could respond.

"We can tell the story until it's a legend. The guy who liked the beer so much, he couldn't wait 'til we opened, instead came through the skylight. Come on, let's get these kegs loaded."

They left me not knowing whether to laugh or be shocked. Maybe I was taking this too seriously. Mo seemed to see opportunities in anything that happened, turning tragedy into a marketing opportunity. I wondered what he had in terms of a graphic. A shadow figure on the floor? It wasn't a bad idea.

I walked outside. Johnny and Brindisi were standing near the hole in the roof, the latter looking a little shaky with the height.

"Who did this job?" Johnny yelled. "A drunk? They didn't even seal the edges."

The comment reminded me of some of the work Nate had done near the end of the build out. He had relied on a couple friends and while he checked the work done inside thoroughly, he mustn't have been so meticulous about the exterior. Doors, skylights, I wondered what else needed repair. Johnny, who at the time had been unsuccessfully trying to get hired at the brewery, would play this well; he never stopped reminding us how hard it had been for him to get a job with the company. He was right, of course, but at the time Nate had seen him as young and unproven.

The two climbed down from the roof. I looked at the sky. "At least it doesn't look like rain."

"Not until the end of the week," said Brindisi.

"Who's using the pickup?" Johnny asked.

"Mel's got kegs to deliver," I said. "What do you need?"

"I want to get started on this today. I need to get some lumber, and you need to order a good window, one made in the U.S."

"Do they still make them here?" Brindisi chimed in.

Johnny held out his hand. In it were several broken screws. "I can tell you one thing. These screws aren't made here. They're all over the roof, half of 'em broken. That's Chinese shit."

While we stood and pondered our manufacturing crisis, the door to the loading dock opened and Melanie and Mo appeared, ready to load kegs.

"I can bike down to the lumber yard, but I'll need the pickup to get the materials," Johnny said.

"I can see you have work to do," Brindisi said. "You've got my card. I'd appreciate any further information you can get me."

"I'll give you a call," I repeated.

Meanwhile, Johnny had walked away, his cell phone to his ear.

I stood and gazed at the roof. The tile job was fine, it was really just the skylight, a last minute addition. But given the breakage, it wouldn't be an easy job to fit another light in there.

Johnny returned. "I got a friend coming over who's got a truck. Said for a case of beer he'll help me pick stuff up at the lumberyard."

"Give him two cases," I said, relieved. 'Three if he can find nails made in the U.S."

"Yeah, right," Johnny replied.

14

When I arrived at the brewery that morning, Mo's car was outside. I imagined Johnny's bike was in the brewery as he rarely allowed our brewer to arrive first, a competitive game he played that meant little to our brewer.

Stepping through the door, I wondered what newly urgent task we'd face. A broken machine, a bar owner needing assistance, a shipment delay—a day rarely passed without something unexpected adding to the usual array of chores to accomplish.

Nate used to say that you peel off the layer of urgent things to tackle and you reveal another layer of urgent things to tackle. If left undone, that second layer of urgencies gets pushed further down the list by other urgencies. Still in its infancy, the microbrewing industry exemplified this. It was a work in progress and relied on people who were new to it, owners finding their way by trial and error. I reminded myself that unlike many businesses, Callahans had a consistently hard-working staff. And that I had complete trust in them.

In the middle of the floor, below the skylight through which Brinkworth had fallen, someone had started to sketch a figure. The words Dead Lawyer IPA were lightly inscribed around it. One of Mo's artist friends had gotten right to work. As with many new ventures, budding artists played a significant role in our startup. Mo knew a lot of them who worked for beer, something we could afford. "They do it for the fame," he maintained.

I thought about our brewer. Undoubtedly the most creative family member, Mo provided a constant flow of ideas. Nate had warned me to rein in the more far-fetched ones as unworkable for our market. While respecting Mo as a malt magician and hop fanatic rolled into one, Nate claimed he'd spent too much time in the vanguard region of microbrewing, the Pacific-Northwest. The Northeast was different, not as experimental in its preferences.

When I first took the reins of Callahans, I worried about how Mo, who I didn't know beyond a few stories Nate had related, would take to me. To my surprise, he flourished. He found Nate too conservative. "Instead of challenging our customers, Nate looked at industry sales figures and pushed beers that sold well but weren't creative. We need the creative side. The risk takers will advance this industry. Risk is essential and you understand that."

What Mo called creative and risky was simply me letting him have his head. He knew much more than I did about the industry. While I had traveled to the west coast numerous times and sampled beer there, he had lived it. The blend of Nate's tendencies with mine worked well.

I'd also quickly seen that the skinny white Rasta look-a-like could brew. And wasn't afraid to share his knowledge. Unlike European brewers, who guarded their centuries long techniques, American brewers shared almost everything. And with Nate gone, Mo had turned up the dial several clicks.

The door opened, Melanie's arrival interrupting my thoughts. She was dressed to work. "What's the plan this morning?"

"I just got here myself," I replied. "But I'm sure Mo's got it all planned."

"I hope so, I gave up a chance to race today."

"You run?"

"No, I've been driving stock since I was twelve. My dad taught me."

"So I should be letting you do the driving when we deliver."

"If you want to get somewhere quickly."

"There you are!" Mo interrupted our conversation, appearing across the floor, wide-eyed and sporting his red, green and gold "Wellies," the English muck boot popularized by the Duke of Wellington. Normally black, Wellies had become standard wear for many brewers. Mo wore "Steel Pulsed" ones, which fit well with his dread locks and island style clothing. They were steel toed.

"Almost got busted last night," Mo said, timing his sentence with Johnny's entrance. "Flex over there was drinking a Bud and we got stopped by the Po-Po."

"'Nother fuckin' dream," Johnny replied, flexing his upper torso.

Mo continued, unflustered. "He stuck the can of swill in my hands just as Mr. Law Enforcement came to the window. The guy asks me if I've been drinking and I say 'Hell no! I don't drink this stuff!' If it had been a barley wine or something, I would have had some difficulty explaining myself, but when I told him I brewed here he recognized me. And let me go."

"Earth to Mo, bring the shuttle in for landing." Johnny shook his head. "Where he comes up with this stuff I don't know. I'm guessing it's the weed."

"I told muscle beach over there I have a reputation to uphold!"

"Did we get the new kegs yet?" I interrupted.

Mo nodded. "Came beginning of the week."

"That's a hell of a pile," Melanie said. "I didn't know we'd had so many accounts."

"Three per knob," Mo said.

"Seems like a lot."

"One for the tap, one for the bar cooler so we don't lose the knob, and one ready and waiting for delivery."

"Most bars don't have the cooler space," Melanie said.

Mo shrugged. "Doesn't change the dynamic. Let's get the line ready."

Mo had been friends with Nate during his college years. He was Nate's walk on the wild side, when my brother had let his hair grow and done most of his pre-career carousing. It was Mo who had convinced Nate to start the brewery. He'd moved to the west coast, where the microbrewery movement had first taken hold, and Nate visited him often, timing his trips between the drug tests he'd taken while climbing the corporate ladder.

I remembered the very moment Nate decided to build the brewery. He'd just come back from visiting Mo and we invited him to dinner. He'd been dating Jenna at the time and the four of us were sitting over dinner, drinking beer. Nate had brought some new beers from his visit, from a brewery called Grant's. The brewery was named after its founder in Yakima, a hop growing region of the Pacific Northwest. We were wowed.

"I'm gonna make this," Nate had declared. "I'm sick of selling for other people."

When Nate said something, he usually meant it, but we all thought his fantasies had taken over his mind. Within a year from that dinner, however, he had quit his job with a large brokerage firm, pooled his money, bought the brewery where I now stood and had flown Mo back from Seattle.

Nate later told me that the money he'd saved was key. At the time the industry was seeing a few major bankruptcies and banks willing to invest in this type of venture had dwindled. He hadn't needed them.

"Who's today's Usher?" Mo asked, interrupting my thoughts.

"That's me." Melanie stepped up.

At Callahans, kegging beer involved four people. On the front end, the Usher would gather the needies and confirm that they were viable—especially that the spindle hadn't broken inside. After an exterior cleaning and scrubbing away any residue around the outlet, the needies were passed to the cleaner/filler.

Each keg held fifteen and a half gallons of beer, or in brewers terms, one half of a barrel. We thought in terms of pints, one hundred and twenty-four if the pour was good, something rare at a bar. The kegs were made of stainless steel, making them costly. Since we owned our kegs, keeping track of them was an operation in itself, starting with the Usher stripping them of any stray labeling that had appeared in the jumble of distribution. We had spray-painted a giant purple C on each of our kegs.

"I'll clean and fill," Johnny said. He looked at Mo. "You Eskimo. Maybe the cooler will chill you out."

Mo nodded. "Ed, you're the Scribe."

"Sounds familiar," I replied.

I admired the organization of our kegging operation. It could actually be performed by two people, even one, but Nate insisted that everyone participate. He sensed the importance of seeing—and blessing—the final product before it was unleashed into the market. More importantly, he'd made this our communication time, when sales staff relayed field information to brewery workers and vice versa. Our brewer needed to know what customers and bar owners were saying about the beer. About how new accounts treated the product, and what was being done to promote each beer. In turn, Mo talked about the beer and what adjustments, if any, he'd made. He tossed out new ideas during these work sessions. Lastly, it was a chance for Johnny to note issues with the brewing equipment so the operation would run more smoothly. Nate preferred these working sessions over everyone sitting around a table.

Because Nate had made kegging beer an all hands on the floor operation, it served as an important bonding time. I had always loved our staff's camaraderie, something characteristic of the industry. Brewery owners and brewers were as distinct as their beer, but remarkably cooperative.

The sound of metal clanging onto the floor indicated that Melanie was ready. The first Needie shot across the floor to Johnny, who stopped it with one foot and turned on the machine. Mo retreated to the cooler while Johnny upended the keg onto the washer. I wheeled the chalkboard from its spot near the door, ready to record ideas and tasks that would arise from the operation.

"I like the outline," I said, once the operation had begun. I had begun to see its marketing potential.

"It'll cost us a keg of beer, when it's finished."

"Good price."

We worked in silence for a while, Melanie scrubbing and Johnny stacking kegs for an easier transfer while I labeled the caps that would enclose the keg outlets.

Mo returned from the cooler. "You still on for brewing next week, Ed?"

I nodded.

"We're brewing Copper. Can't run out of the cash cow."

"And me?" Melanie stopped cleaning and looked at Mo.

"What about you?" asked Mo.

"When do I get to brew?"

"I thought you knew beer."

"I do. And you say I have a good palate. But I don't know the process. I'm sure that would help me sell."

"He ain't gonna teach you nothin'," Johnny said.

"Bar owners are impressed when a woman knows more than they do," Mel said.

"You're welcome to come."

"Let me know what day," Melanie said, returning her attention to the keg she was cleaning.

15

I made the turn on lap 40, having decided that another five would do me good. What I loved about swimming was its solitary nature. You were alone in the water, unaware even of the person in the next lane over. Sure there had been the fans yelling in the background—parents mostly— but they were easy to tune out. Even during the team races I swam alone, focusing on form and speed to the exclusion of everything else. Now I was less concerned about the contests and focused on extending my distance while using the time for reflection.

I remembered something Nate had said before he died, about why he knew the brewery would succeed. He said we made a great team. He had the impetuousness to get something started and I had the long term guts to keep it going. It surprised me that he doubted his ability to keep a business going, but he claimed he lacked confidence—something rare for him—in anything long term. I think his relationships with women gave him this idea. Jenna was just one of his failures. In our lighter moments we used to joke that he'd bedded enough women to start a mid-sized city, but I know he envied what I had found in Sarah. And of course I'd kid him about being such a loser with women.

I turned another lap as thoughts of what had happened at the brewery filled my mind. I needed to sort out the facts before seeing Sarah. Stan's crash and the fact that we knew nothing beyond that it might not have been an accident. The guy in Sam's who claimed Tony Wehrmann was a killer. A fruitless search for a broken tail light in the Wehrmann truck lot. A dead street lamp done by someone with a sophisticated tool. And now a death in the brewery, with a man carrying a gun.

The gun stuck in my mind. What had Brinkworth been doing with it? Was he bringing it to me, and if so, why? If not, why was he holding it in his hand? Was it something dug up from his past? He and I didn't have much of a past.

Brinkworth wasn't from the university, though it was understandable why Sarah had thought that. He was the lead lawyer for the state's attempt to close an old landfill. According to who spoke, he had been many things: an honest bureaucrat doing his job to shut down a community hazard; an overly ambitious lawyer trying to leverage a big case into the Commissioner's seat; or simply a guy in over his head. I knew him as someone who drank too much and talked too freely. But that was after the case, which he'd lost.

I first saw him when I brought my Human Ecology class into a courtroom to witness environmental law in action. The state wanted to close the Sand Ridge Landfill, due to allegations of illegal dumping. Sand Ridge was also atop an aquifer, and leaching could endanger the community's water supply. Even without the allegations, it should have been an open and shut case. But Brinkworth botched it. He'd taken the case personally, letting emotion and rhetoric assume front seat. Instead of illuminating the dangers to the community simply by presenting facts, he'd gone on an emotional rant. In the end, realizing he had lost, he'd started weeping, right in the courtroom. That was when I made the decision to go to the newspaper with my research.

After the trial, I lost touch with him. Nate's death and taking over the brewery took me on a different course. Brinkworth had shown up there, but even when he came to buy beer he'd never said much. He didn't even stay to sample our new offerings. He was a Copper drinker and that was it. Nor had he formed a bond with the brewery staff like many of the regulars did. Perhaps that's why his loss didn't seem great to us.

Back on the breast stroke, I gazed at the bottom of the pool as I swam. A patchwork of light moved against the turquoise basin. It was a comfortable feeling for me, so familiar in the countless pools where I had swum. Or was it the pond? I had learned to swim at a small pond near our house, taking Nate with me. I had always begun by swimming far out, only stopping after Nate had turned back. He often said that my pushing him until he couldn't swim any farther had made him a better athlete.

Except the back stroke. I didn't do the back stroke no matter how many times my coaches pushed me. The thought of staring at the ceiling or sky frightened me. Something nameless, dreadful. I quit the school team my senior year. The coaches tried to push me to dive, but I didn't want to swim competitively any more.

Another turn, another lap as I headed toward the finish. I felt strong. I hadn't told Brindisi about my trip to the Wehrmann truck lot. I wasn't sure why. Perhaps because it wasn't legal. Or that I didn't want any more trouble. Someone getting killed at the brewery, no matter what the reason, was not good. We could only have so many Dead beers even though I'm sure Mo would love a Dead Distributor Ale.

Once again, the thought occurred to me that I was in over my head. A little back-stabbing around the university was one thing, but someone crashing through the brewery roof holding a gun was serious. He must have seen cars in the parking lot so why hadn't he knocked? Or had he been up there when people arrived this morning?

Lap 45, finished. I touched the pool's side and stood, then pulled my swim goggles off. Leaving the pool I grabbed my towel and nodded to the life guard sitting lazily in her chair. She smiled. Easiest job in the world, I remembered. The hardest part was staying awake when there was no one in the pool.

It wasn't until I reached the pickup and saw the six-pack in the passenger seat that I remembered to visit Sam. Sales was still the difficult part of this business. Nate made it seem easy. All his life he'd been able to get a conversation going even if it was to tell the same story repeatedly. He was a natural. I had to search for something to say and silence made it more difficult. In normal conversations, this was no problem, but in sales you had to keep the conversation going. And gauge when your customers had heard enough.

I'd had this discussion with Nate before he died. He said I was a born listener and that was just as good a way to engage and sell beer. We'd gone out together a few times once the brewery was running and he'd watched me. He'd nicknamed me The Counselor, saying that unlike many people who went to bars and found someone to talk to in the bartender, I was the opposite. Before I'd finished my first pint, I'd have bartenders telling *me* their woes.

The bar was busy when I arrived. Sam was serving several customers and carrying on conversations. He was in his element and through my first pint I simply sat and admired a master at work, bringing a plateful of cheer to each customer. His usual delivery line, "So tell me how your day's been goin'," seemed to get most people talking.

We needed to cement a knob at this bar. Customers hung on Sam's every word and if those words were good things said about our beers, it would create more Callahan beer drinkers.

I set my empty pint glass down and Sam noticed. He motioned to the six-pack on the bar for him.

"I'll have the Pilsner," I said.

"Got it. That the sample you brought?" I nodded. "Bring me a keg tomorrow."

"You don't want to try it?"

"I already have." He smiled at my blank look. "You didn't think I wasn't going to do some research, did you? I bought a six-pack. It's a good beer."

"Thank you," I replied. "I'll make sure my brewer hears that."

"The Porter should kick in the next couple days," he replied. "I'll put your stout on there. Gotta have a dark beer on tap as the weather cools."

"Thank you," I repeated, unable to come up with anything else to say.

"Your new employee was in here the other night," Sam said.

"Melanie?" I fought the quick note of annoyance I felt that she thought I needed help.

"Yeah. She came in with a bunch of her friends. She knows beer."

"Where's Lenny?" I asked, deciding to change the subject and perhaps get some more information out of Sam.

He shrugged. "Haven't seen him in a few days."

"He must have some interesting stories," I remarked, trying to remain casual.

"What do you mean?"

"About Iraq."

"He was never in Iraq," Sam replied.

"I thought he said he…"

"He *said*," Sam interrupted. "Trust me, Lenny's never been to Iraq. He's probably never been off the east side. He likes to tell stories, makes them up from conversations he has with the customers that come in."

I shrugged, filing this piece of information with the others. His story of Tony Wehrmann was just that, a story.

Halfway through my beer, I saw a Wehrmann Brothers rep arrive. Sam took the six-pack of Callahan's Stout off the bar top and set it in the lower cooler. I finished my beer, thanked him, and left, promising to bring the keg by tomorrow while wondering if moving the six-pack had been coincidental.

As I walked toward my car, I thought about the coming day. We were brewing. I noticed the Wehrmann delivery truck out front, backed in next to my pickup. On a chance, I walked around to the front. The right turn signal cover was missing and there was a dent in the fender.

16

"Was it the same one?"

"Yes."

"How did you know?"

"I compared them."

"How?"

"I had the one I picked up at the scene of the accident in the pickup. I got it and compared it with the unbroken light."

Sarah licked her fingers. We sat in bed, eating chocolate and drinking strong black coffee. It was Sunday afternoon and we had just made love, something we always did when one of us returned from out of town. The hour didn't matter, the intimacy did.

"So what's for dinner?" Sarah asked.

"I was thinking we'd start with shrimp Caesar salad. Lobster for the main course, boiled and served with hot butter."

"Mmm, hot."

"Who, me?"

"The lobster."

I kissed her. "Nothing more on the case?" I had related everything I knew. She'd already heard about Brinkworth's death but I filled in the details on that, too.

"I think I've got enough to work on," she replied.

"It's funny, while in the pool Friday I was thinking about swimming with Nate when we were kids."

"What about?"

"Just how I used to swim until he'd turn back. And how once we got older and he could keep up, I'd take him to the other side of the pond, where the factory overflow pipes were. After a big rain we'd swim against the flow; I think I got my swimming strength from that. How was I to know that was when they released chemical waste?"

"You're still blaming yourself."

"How was I to know?" I repeated.

"It could have been anything that killed Nate. That's what the doctors said. Anything."

I didn't respond.

"Get that thought out of your head," Sarah continued. "You were kids and you didn't know what was going on at the factory. You might just as well blame your dad. He worked there."

"Right," I replied quickly. "What do you think I should do about this turn signal?"

"Nothing."

"Nothing?"

"It's over. If something happened, it did. Just keep your eyes open."

"Do you think it had any connection to Brinkworth?"

Sarah shook her head. "You lead such a dangerous life, dear." She smiled. "And I think you're connecting coincidental dots."

I wasn't convinced. "I asked Johnny to check out the list of trucks that have that style turn signal. In case the one I saw at Sam's is unique. It would seal the case."

"So how is work beyond the great mystery? Is everyone taking the accident okay?"

"They're fine, Mo even named a beer after the guy, Dead Lawyer."

"That's creative. Will it sell?"

"Bigger question is if it will get past the regulators. I imagine a few lawyers will have to look at it. Nate always worried about that."

"Hence the conservative names on the beers."

I nodded. "Funny, we still talk about him every day. He's our inspiration. I feel like I'm constantly being compared to him and what he would do in every situation." I hesitated, then added, "Not in a bad way."

"I think he was pretty confident in the guy he turned the business over to," Sarah said. "I know I am. And you hated the university job."

"I loved it in many ways, just couldn't handle the bullshit."

"I know what you mean."

"You've managed pretty well," I said.

"I know, but there's nothing worse than being smarter than your boss."

"I keep reminding myself that. But the best is not having a boss. Although I do feel that the investors, despite being friends, are bosses. Always having to keep an eye on where the money is going."

"You're lucky you have Jenna," Sarah said. "She's a whiz at that."

"She's taken on a lot. She's got Junior, Stan in a wheelchair, and now she's taking on the books. All this with a full-time job; I hope it's not too much."

"I think she knows the nature of small business ownership."

"I'd love to be able to bring her on full time, if she'd give up her job."

"How is Stan doing?" Sarah asked.

"Says he wants to come back. We'd have to rearrange the office."

"Will you give him back all his accounts?"

"I'm going to let he and Melanie decide. Stan's good at opening new places, he's just like Nate."

"Two peas in a pod."

"Melanie's no slouch, either. She got our beer into Sam's and cemented knobs at several other places."

"That's good to hear. Can the books afford an additional sales person?"

"If they keep selling. One thing I've learned is that you never want to let a good salesman go. Never. He might go and work for the competition. Or she," I added.

Sarah smiled at my use of the female gender. In the male-dominated world of the beer business, I was learning.

The next morning I received my monthly call from John Biers, the city editor and reporter for the local paper. He had convinced his boss to allow him to write a monthly column about beer and often quoted me for the column.

I had known John—whose last name was celebrated by all of us—since well before Nate began the brewery. He had originally written about environment issues, but with the downsizing that had occurred at the city daily, had taken on several other beats. Beer reporting was his favorite.

This morning he wanted to talk about the movement toward craft beer. I told him he'd get more info from Mo, who was better versed in the topic.

"You have a better conceptual mind, John. Mo just does what he does but isn't as able to explain the picture."

"I guess that's a good clue to how it all happened," I replied. "If you look at the different success stories in this industry, it reminds me of a new art form, where these guys—and gals although there are few of them in this industry—went out and did things without thinking too much. They learned the trade, got creative, and people responded."

"The failures? The papers are full of talk about them these days."

"Hype. Microbrewed beer isn't going away. The losers mostly lack creativity, passion, and the drive to succeed," I said. "The past few years everyone and their mother thought it was easy money to make beer. The ones that will thrive are in it for the long haul. The ones thinking it's a path to riches will mostly fail."

"You're a regular beer Nostradamus."

"Then there's the beer drinker," I added, warming to the topic like I was back in a classroom in front of rapt students. "They've been introduced to options. Today's beer drinkers, the core of our consumer base, are inspired by what's on the shelves."

"Not like when we were young."

I agreed. "Our choices were quite limited. Today's game is to keep the young beer drinker interested in your product. There isn't the loyalty to a brewery that was common in our time."

"Why is that?"

"Many reasons. The big old regionals used to employ a lot of people and those employees created centers of loyalty for the jobs they held. With the growth of huge, national brands, this mostly disappeared, or certainly shrunk. Then there is quality. While no one will beat Anheuser-Busch in quality control and ingredients, for example, their beers are geared to the taste of the mass beer drinker. Like the McDonald's of beer. Keeping that consistency is essential to their business and they do a great job at it.

"The small places have to win customers on more than the freshness of a local product and an uncle who makes his living from the business. They have to up the flavor and creativity of what they make. It's a craft and a challenge.

Part of the reason we've seen the flattening of sales today is small breweries' inability to maintain a high level of quality. There is still a lot of mediocre beer out there claiming to be an upscale product."

"What about distribution?" John asked, knowing how I felt about that topic.

"It's outdated. You have these giant companies—many of them still family-owned—who used to work with even larger brewing companies. The laws were written to protect them, rightfully so. Now they're being asked to work with many small companies and balance that work with the fact that they are making their living distributing a big company's beer."

"Sounds like an opportunity for a small business."

"I agree. Smaller distributorships are badly needed. It's not an easy business, working on small margins, but it's a big opportunity. Until we see someone like that here, we'll stick to self-distribution." I hesitated, then asked, "Aren't you going to ask me about the death at the brewery?

"No. The city desk is covering that. I'm more interested in the bigger picture. And you and I know where the Brinkworth thing may lead. He never really got over losing the state's case to close the Sand Ridge Landfill."

17

I arrived at the brewery earlier than usual the next morning. The front door was open and Johnny was already at work. Surprisingly—again—so was Mo. They were in the office.

"Here he is, ask him," Mo said as I entered.

"What?" I asked.

Johnny looked a little embarrassed, then blurted, "You doin' her?"

"*What?*"

"The girl you hired. You doin' her?"

"You mean Melanie?"

He nodded.

Mo leaned back in his chair. "Johnny has a little trouble getting beyond 'she' and 'her' when he talks about women. I keep telling him, he's never going to get anywhere until he starts learning names."

"I get more than…" Johnny began.

"Wait," I interrupted. "To respond to your question, no, obviously. Melanie works here. She was a student of mine for God's sake."

"It's ain't like that don't happen. You been hanging at night with her, too. And she likes you." He held out his hands, palms up, as if this was all self explanatory.

"The guy sounds like your wife," Mo interjected.

I shook my head. "Get that out of your head. Melanie is here because she's a good employee."

"Okay," Johnny said. He seemed satisfied.

I waited a moment, then asked, "What brought this on?"

"I was asking knucklehead over there if she was single," Johnny replied. "She doesn't seem to be hanging out with anyone 'cept you."

"Why don't you ask her?"

"What happened to that older woman you were dating?" Mo interjected. "What was her name, Jane, Joan, Jeri…"

"Joanne," Johnny said. "She was too old. I told her it was over."

"Bummer," Mo said. "How many IBUs?"

"Over 100," Johnny said.

"100 IBUs!" Mo replied in disbelief.

"*Over* 100."

"What do IBUs have to do with this?" I asked.

"Bitterness Units," Johnny said. "Something we counted when Nate was around."

"What's the I stand for?" I asked.

"International," Mo said, letting the front legs of his chair fall to the floor. "Bitterness crosses borders." He looked at Johnny. "You really think it was 100 IBUs?"

Johnny flexed. "She liked me. It was *at least* 100 IBUs."

Melanie entered the office.

"Be careful, Mel," Mo said. "Johnny's on the prowl and he's just left *another* woman."

"I heard," she said. "100 IBUs is angry. I only came that close once."

"Who'd you break up with?" Johnny asked.

"I didn't," she replied. "He left me."

"Someone left you?" Johnny said. "Stupid."

Melanie smiled at him. "Thanks. It happens to the best of us. I learned a good lesson."

"This isn't some kind of meeting with the boss again, is it?" I asked, suddenly suspicious with the three of them in the office.

Mo shook his head. "No, I came early to work on Dead Lawyer. Still not satisfied with the hop profile. Needs a little more bitterness."

"Speaking of Dead Lawyer, give me some info so I can sell it," Melanie said.

"I bet he's got a slogan all picked out," Johnny said.

"I do," Mo said. "It's an IPA, because like lawyers, everyone has to have one. *And* everyone wishes them ill." Mo stood. "What's that line from Shakespeare, first let's kill all the lawyers."

"And then go have a beer," Johnny finished.

"I can see it now," I said. "Let's all toast a Dead Lawyer. I like the floor outline. Turned out nice."

"Don't worry about specs, the beer will sell itself," Mo said.

"The bigger question is whether you should brew another batch right away," I said. "We don't want to run out."

"Brew day is Wednesday."

"We'll be there."

"Grain shipment arrives today. That'll give me three, four weeks to turn it around."

"How do you determine the IBUs of a Dead Lawyer?" I asked, pleased with my cleverness.

"I think in this case it's no different than a relationship," Mo replied. "The key is to avoid becoming collateral damage. Like those reporters last week, they all wanted a piece of me for their story. I had to slip out the back."

"Like in a relationship?" Melanie said. "Now you're sounding like the Mo I know."

Mo shrugged, then picked up his glass and focused on the beer sample in front of him. "I'm not sure I like the color. Clarity is fine, but I want it a shade lighter."

"For a minute I thought we were talking about relationships," Melanie said.

"They're exhausting," Mo replied, looking up from his beer. "It's like dodging bullets."

"That's what it takes to be a stud," Johnny said.

"You used to say that was fun," Melanie replied.

"On the front end it's exciting," Mo said.

Johnny shook his head slowly. "Nate would be disappointed. Like he said, just think every moment is fourth down of the fourth quarter."

"At my age, it becomes tiring more quickly. Has anyone tried the latest Barrels beer?" Mo asked, referring to our local competitor. "They're calling it an English IPA."

"Had it last night," Melanie said.

"I had it," Johnny added.

"What did you think?"

"Tastes like home brew," Johnny said.

Melanie was silent and Mo continued. "It was too sweet. Lingered too long on the palate, a little cloying. Maybe version two will be drier."

"You say that about every beer," Johnny replied. "I don't think you're ever had a beer that's too dry or too bitter. Just like your life."

"Good one, ace," Mo replied. "That's called a refined palate. You'll get there someday."

"I'll stick with the Copper," Johnny replied. "Meanwhile, I got work to do. I'm goin' up on the roof and get that frame ready. The window's comin' today."

"Do you need help?" I asked.

"I'll call when I do."

"I need to speak with you after you get that framed in," I said. He nodded and left.

"I still need specs," Melanie persisted. "IBUs, O.G., percent alcohol."

"What a beer geek you are," Mo said.

"I'm going out today and want to sell the entire batch."

"Such impatience."

Melanie looked at me and shrugged. "I can't sell what I don't know."

"Save one for Sam," I said. "Speaking of which, thanks for your help with him, Mel. I went to give him a sample six-pack and he ordered a keg, said you were in there with friends."

"Yeah, they dragged me out. I said I'd only go if they went to a bar with good beer. They let me choose."

"Well, thanks. I'm sure I could have done it without you, but the help is appreciated."

"So what's your favorite beer?" Melanie asked.

"Why?"

"I owe you a case. You won the bet."

"Does it still count if you helped me?"

"Of course it does."

"I have trouble picking a favorite beer. Sometimes it's a stout, sometimes an IPA. I also like sours."

"A vinegar head," Mo said. "In that case go for the expensive one, like Cantillon Iris, at thirty-two dollars a bottle."

"I have to go with an American beer," I said. "Support the industry."

"There are plenty of expensive beers in the U.S.," Melanie said.

I excused myself and walked outside. Johnny was about ready to climb the ladder to the roof. "Need help yet?" I asked.

He shook his head. "Hey, sorry about what I said about Melanie. That what you wanted to talk to me about?"

"No," I replied, noting that he'd actually used her name and thinking that was a good thing. "She is a good looking woman, but too young for me."

"I got you mixed up with Nate. He would have been all over that."

"He wasn't stupid enough to mix it up with an employee," I said.

Johnny shrugged, as if unconvinced. "So what did you want?"

"You remember that turn signal I gave you a while ago?" He nodded again. "What'd you find out?"

"Standard for a box van."

"What brand?"

"There's a list."

"Do you have a list?"

"I can get one. Where on my list of priorities do you want me to put it?"

"Get that window framed and sealed first," I replied.

"I did find out about the street light. Found the tool lying nearby in the grass."

"Can we get fingerprints?" I asked.

"Wasn't thinking along those lines," Johnny said. "It's probably got mine all over it."

18

The reggae was turned up loud when I arrived the next morning, and that meant Mo was ready to brew. I had long since given up asking him to turn down the noise, pointing to the vibrating windows in the old building as a potential safety issue. Good music made the beer good, Mo insisted, and whether it was superstition or not, I wouldn't interfere with his magic.

Melanie, Johnny, and Mo were in the office when I entered.

"The roof looks great," I said.

"Thanks, I still have some finishing framing to do," Johnny said.

"You sure it won't leak?" Mo asked.

Johnny gave Mo a look of disdain. "You don't know how lucky you are to have me—and at my slave wage."

"Welcome to the small brewery industry; slave wages are how we stay in business," Mo said. "But it's still better than what you were doing."

Johnny looked pained.

"Tell Mel what you were doing before you got your slave wage job here," Mo said.

"It's not relevant," Johnny said.

"What were you doing?" Melanie asked.

"Tell her." Johnny remained silent, and Mo added, "He was digging shit holes."

"Fuck off," Johnny said.

"It's true," Mo continued. "He worked for a septic tank company, digging holes for new builds. Giant holding tanks for shit."

"What's wrong with that?" Melanie said.

"You're right, someone's got to make room for all the shit," Mo said.

"No, I mean it's a living," Melanie said. "And I'll bet a lot of hard work. I'm impressed." Melanie held out her hands. "Let me see your hands."

Embarrassed, Johnny held out his hands.

"Strong," she said

"It was hard work," Johnny said, "Harder than repairing a skylight."

"I'll bet," she said, letting his hands go.

"And Lou was never happy. I'd dig a huge hole and he'd say, 'Not big enough. See how the edges slope inward as you get deeper? Needs to be straight down to fit the tank.'"

"So that's where you got your perfectionist streak," I said.

"Digging shit holes," Mo added.

Johnny laughed. "Where the first beers you brewed should have gone, right into one of those shit holes."

"Ow," said Mo. "Time to brew."

Minutes later, Mel and I joined our brewer on the brewing system platform, dressed and booted.

"Let's start with ingredients," Mel said. "What are we talking about?"

"I thought you knew all that," Mo said.

"I'm a taster, not a brewer," Mel replied.

"Then let's start at the beginning. Beer is made from four ingredients. Water, malt, hops, and yeast." Mo picked up a vial of malt, which he used when giving brewery tours. "Malt is the sugar that will ferment into the alcohol we know and love.

"The sugars come from barley," he continued, holding out his hand. "Try it."

Mel and I took a few grains and ate them.

"Sweet," Mel said.

"Raw barley isn't this sweet," Mo said. "In order to get the sweetness, the maltster tricks the grain—which you know as a seed—into starting to grow. He wets the grains, making them think spring is here and it's time to sprout. The un-sweet proteins of the grain are converted to starches thusly."

"What about the enzymes?" Mel asked. "I thought they were part of this."

"We'll get to that, but let's do the basics first. Once the grains start to sprout, the maltster heats them, stopping the process and giving us malt."

"Hey knucklehead, you want the hops yet?"

Mo ignored Johnny's catcall and continued. "We put the malt into our mash tun and soak them in hot water." He pointed to one of the two large vessels of the brewhouse platform. "This is where enzymes come in, Mel, finishing the process by converting our starches into fermentable sugars, called wort. Spelled or, pronounced er."

Johnny climbed the stairs on the platform and set down a pail onto the platform. "Hops for the boil," he said.

"Thanks, champ." Mo pointed to the mash tun. "I started the process this morning, so I'm ready to transfer the wort."

"How thoughtful," Mel said.

"The guy's full of thoughts," Johnny said.

"The mash is ready to transfer," Mo said, ignoring Johnny. He turned back to the brewing system and switched on a pump. "I'll pump the liquid into the kettle, where we'll boil it and add the third ingredient, hops."

"The first two ingredients being water and malt," I said.

"Very good, professor," Mo replied.

"Ed, can I speak with you?" I turned to find Jenna behind me. I looked at Mo.

"Transfer is going to take a while," he said.

"This won't take long," Jenna said.

I closed the office door. "How's Stan?"

"Aching to get back to work," she replied.

"What do the doctors say?"

"A couple weeks, but he won't be doing any heavy lifting. And he'll have to keep a rigid physical therapy schedule."

"It'll still be good to get him back." I touched her shoulder. "I appreciate your taking over the books. It's never been my strong suit."

"That's what I wanted to talk to you about."

"Is something wrong?"

"We're losing money. I had to move some of Nate's savings into our operating account to pay the bills."

"We're selling more beer than ever," I said, at the same time glad that Nate had signed over money management privileges to Jenna.

"And it's costing more than ever. I still don't have a handle on it, but paying staff, taxes, insurance, and a host of other costs—not to mention brewing ingredients—has taken its toll."

"Should I lay Melanie off?"

"No!" Jenna replied quickly.

"We can't raise our keg price. We're already higher than Barrels."

"Let me work with what we have and see where we can cut," Jenna finished. "I just wanted you to be the first to know. Now I gotta get back to work."

When I returned to the brewhouse, Mo had entranced Mel and Johnny with a story I'd already heard, about his attempts to register the name Bottoms Up for a beer. I half-listened, numbed from my conversation with Jenna.

"So I ask him, 'Can you tell me what the approval status is on the label we sent?' I get a long silence, then, 'It's been rejected.'

"I ask why and he says the label is too suggestive.

"'What do you mean?' I ask.

"'You have the name Bottoms Up, which is bad enough. Then you have the woman's derriere, which is too obvious. It's leading.'"

"He said derriere?" Johnny asked.

Mo nodded, and continued. "'What about the man's derriere?' I ask. "He tells me man's derriere is fine."

"He said that," Johnny interjected, dubious.

Mo nodded again. "So I say, 'I mean what about the fact that there is also a man on the label?'

"'It's not the man. It's the woman's bottom. It's too large.'

"'So if I just shave something off her derriere, you'll approve it?'

"'I can't promise you anything,' he tells me. 'My suggestion is do without the derriere.'"

"I can see things have gone downhill," I said, pushing Jenna's news away for the moment.

Mo climbed the platform and looked into the mash tun. "All set," he said. "Now we got to bring this baby to a boil. You guys want to shovel out some spent grain?"

19

"I had another dream last night." I rolled onto my back. Sarah was standing at the mirror, *en prepario finito* as I called the last movements of her getting ready for work, something I'd never tire of watching. Light touches put her hair in place, a tissue removed the tiny smudge of eye brow liner, a brush caressed the light coating of foundation.

"I'm surprised," she replied, turning. "It didn't seem like you slept at all. You were tossing and turning."

"Nate and I were at the pond," I continued. "We caught a large perch, and not wanting to share it, we started a fire near shore and cooked it. It tasted delicious. I gave Nate most of it."

I could see that Sarah was impatient, ready to head into her world. "We ate quickly, scraping our plates while the pond burned, plumes of black smoke rising from it like the smoke off a car tire—black, tarry, and thick."

"Speaking of eating, I won't be home tonight."

"Another date?"

"A new boyfriend."

"As long as it's another step up that ladder," I said, my usual riposte.

"This one is just for the sex."

"Can I get sloppy seconds when you come home?"

"*If* I come home."

"Tomorrow, then?" After a hesitation, I added, "You can go."

"We'll talk about the dream tonight," Sarah said. She bent to kiss me and left.

"Coffee's ready!" I yelled at a lingering whiff of perfume. Then turned over and closed my eyes. I had an extra thirty minutes this morning. The brewery would be fine while I spoke with Brindisi. He'd called to ask that I stop by the police precinct to answer a few questions.

Instead of sleep, I was transported back to the last weeks of Nate's life. The emotions returned, familiar, intense, crushing. He was being transferred to hospice care; it was just a matter of time. He had asked me to visit him to go over some last minute finances before he died.

At the time I was in the midst of my struggle with the university administration. I had co-published my study of local land contamination, linking it to Guthman Chemical. The press had picked up on the study and as the spokesperson for the study, I'd been interviewed by John Biers on the results. Lawsuits had started.

Nate's condition had worsened. After five years of remission, the cancer had returned with a vengeance. The period when he could hope to survive was over; the fiercest competitor I had ever known was losing his last bout.

I had often said that if ever a person could beat a disease by pure will power, Nate was that person. He had left his therapy groups because they were too fatalistic. He had resumed playing sports, showing even more competitiveness on the field as his body aged. If a positive mindset had anything to do with healing, Nate would have topped the list.

I heard of his progress—or the lack of it—through Sarah, who sat at his side, where I should have been. I was involved in my own struggle, I had told myself. The administration I worked for was scrambling to deal with the damage I had done to their reputation as the local press questioned why they were honoring a company CEO by naming the new Chemistry building after him. Guthman Hall became the scene of a daily protest, the name a symbol of industrial pollution and irresponsibility.

Once the administration had failed to convince me not to publish my research, they iced our relationship. Tenure kept my job safe, but it was obvious that I had stepped over a line—trust, Johnson called it. I became an undesirable.

I hadn't expected the student reaction, had come to see my environmental science class as an exercise in ivory tower activism, dishing out the information universities were so good at doing while doing nothing to foster the activism that should follow the knowledge. And most university kids had little time to pay attention to such a local issue.

I had grown used to teacher/student apathy. Of course there were activists, students who often went on to graduate school given their interest, but never more than a scattered few. Certainly not the group that Melanie had talked about. Maybe she was exaggerating; memories of a fun-filled youth could be polished with an activist deed here and there. But the students had been there every day, sitting on the lawn outside the fencing of the site of new construction. So were the cameras, following the lead of Biers' newspaper articles detailing my research.

When I did visit Nate in his last weeks, my mind was elsewhere, drugged into a state of self-righteous indignation. Tossed onto that pyre was the fact that he was dying from his contact with the same types of chemicals Guthman Corporation had spread across our community. That was the best the doctors could say; conclusive evidence of the precise cause of his cancer was not available. The issue had left the front pages a decade ago.

My focus on the case rather than Nate's predicament, I later realized, was an attempt to deal with his death by placing blame somewhere. I had ignored my brother. He wanted to talk about the brewery, which meant everything to him, and I was skipping that conversation. Sarah told me I was putting principle over people, a euphemistic way of telling me I should focus more on my brother. I didn't even listen.

Somehow, all this seemed like unfinished business. I'd stopped thinking—obsessing, Sarah called it—about this period of my life, pushed into a subconscious part of my brain never to deal with. Rolling over, I decided to get ready for my visit to Brindisi. I wasn't going to be able to sleep.

The police precinct in West District was built in the post WWII years. A low brick structure with an inbuilt, narrow entrance led to a locked door. Once I'd been buzzed in, I sat in one of the few chairs scattered in a spare, unwelcome waiting room. The secretary, after finishing a telephone call that sounded more personal than police-related, signaled me to the counter with a nod. After listening to my quick introduction, she called the back office, then informed me that one of the detectives would see me. I was buzzed through another door and into a long hallway. A number of rooms lead off the hall with low, hung ceilings and fluorescent lights. One of the lights followed me down the hall with a sporadic blinking. The walls were cement block, painted dark gray, and haphazardly decorated with the usual police poster warnings: seat belts, safety precautions, and the importance of traffic signals.

"In here," a voice said, halfway down the hall.

I entered the room and was met by a plain clothes dressed man I didn't recognize. "'Brindi' got held up in traffic," the man said. "Have a seat."

I sat in the chair offered, facing the man, who made an attempt to clear a spot on his desk.

"How can I help you?"

"Officer Brindisi asked to see me."

"Do you know what it was about?"

"No. Is he coming?"

"He'll be here."

"Then maybe while we wait, I can ask if you've made any progress on that accident on Conner's Cliff." As I spoke, I realized how odd I must sound to this man, who hadn't even introduced himself to me. "I'm Ed Callahan, by the way." I stretched out my hand.

"Callahans Copper?" the officer asked, taking my hand.

"Yes."

"I love that beer."

"Officer...?"

"Donnelly. Hey, that's the place where the guy fell through the roof. Was he drinking?"

"Actually, I thought I was here to answer questions about that." I replied.

"Brinkworth was his name, right?"

I nodded.

"Now there was a guy," Donnelly continued. "A local lawyer, working for the state, you'd think he'd be a little smarter, but this guy had harassment suits all over the place."

"Women?" I asked, taken by surprise.

"He was threatening big-wigs. Community leaders. We never did figure out why. He even threatened to kill one guy. We had to bring him in for questioning."

"I'm not sure who you're talking about."

"Some old man who lived up on Snob Hill."

"Guthman?" I barely managed to ask, shocked.

"Guthman, that's it, the guy's name was Arnold Guthman. A harmless old man; Arnie we called him. Seemed nice enough. What's this about Conner's Cliff?"

I was about to answer when Brindisi walked into the room. I stood up and shook his hand.

"You tell him about Brinkworth?" Brindisi asked, continuing the conversation.

"I did."

"I know we went over this before," Brindisi said, "but where were you when Brinkworth died?"

"I was in the office with my employees," I replied, thinking the question strange.

"And you can have someone corroborate that."

"My entire staff."

He leafed through the folder in his hands, still standing. I suddenly wondered if I was a suspect.

"You knew Brinkworth," Brindisi said.

"I did."

"You worked with him?"

"I had some dealings with him in court."

"And you knew Arnold Guthman."

"I don't think his name ever came up before, but I knew of him, didn't know him personally."

"How did you know him?"

"Again, I didn't know him personally. But he was a benefactor of the university where I worked."

"Any reason why Brinkworth would have wanted to kill Guthman?"

"Kill is a pretty strong word," I replied, remembering the courtroom where the lawyer had broken down in front of a judge who refused to allow most of his evidence against the factory owner to be used. Brinkworth's breakdown had botched the case. Or perhaps something else was going on and the case was already moot. "It was complicated," I finished.

"Try to sum it up," Brindisi encouraged.

"I published a study that implicated Guthman's company in the pollution of Skunktown—that's..."

"I know where Skunktown is," Brindisi interrupted, his voice taking on a more impatient tone.

"Brinkworth was the legal counsel attempting to indict the company for the illegal dumping. I was called as a witness."

"Didn't you think it strange?"

"What?"

"That a lawyer would break down like that?" Brindisi sat in the remaining office chair.

"I did. In fact, I told him it jeopardized the case."

"What did he say?"

"He told me to mind my own business, that I was just one witness in a long list. And that he was going to get Guthman if it killed him." There was a silence as I thought about the irony in my statement.

"Did he express any animosity toward Mr. Guthman?"

"Besides calling him a sniveling Judas?"

"And did you have any more contact with Brinkworth after the trial?"

"I saw him at the brewery occasionally, buying beer."

"You didn't talk to him?"

"No, I didn't have anything to say really. I had moved on and I assumed so did he. I could read about the results of the trial in the paper."

Brindisi stood up. "I'll let you know if we need anything else. Officer Donnelly will escort you out."

I left the police station shaken. I had arrived seeking information about Stan's accident, instead had been interrogated about Brinkworth's death. Had Brindisi been watching from behind one of those one way mirrors while Donnelly questioned me? He had changed his tone from the day I spoke to him at the brewery. More brusque and inquisitive. Definitely more suspicious.

Was I a suspect? How could I have pushed someone to their death and been in the office at the same time? Had I hired someone to do this? What had really happened to Brinkworth? It was ten in the morning. Was he already drunk? Had he slipped and fallen? I focused on what was directly in front of me; my periphery held only suspicion.

A pickup truck idled at the curb outside the precinct. Two people sat in it. I remember seeing the pickup when I entered the building. I turned toward my car, my gaze shifting. I walked slowly along the sidewalk, vaguely aware of the pickup. I felt danger—ambiguous, dark, threatening.

As I opened the door to my car, I glanced back. Were they awaiting me? Or was it paranoia? I pulled onto the street and the pickup followed. I took a quick turn off my route into a neighborhood. The street was lined with trees and scattered, street-parked cars. The pickup appeared in my rear view mirror. Unable to think, I pulled to the curb between two cars. The pickup slowed. Then swept by me. As it passed I saw what looked like the barrel of a shotgun poking up from between the passenger's legs. The pickup continued down the street and I sat for a while, paralyzed. I hadn't been able to get a glimpse of either person's face.

Finally, I decided to call the police. While it seemed silly, I couldn't be too careful with something like this and wanted to document anything suspicious. At least I had my peripheral vision back.

20

Munchies had made its name by providing daily finger foods to its patrons. Nothing great, just pre-made pizza squares, fried foods, and a few salty items to elevate customer thirst. For a while the bar had been a rage with the stoner crowd, who would toke up in the parking lot and go in to feed. The local police got wind of this and told the owner, Jim McDavin, to do something. McDavin had placed an employee in the lot to knock on car windows.

Lately, however, the bar featured microbrews with its array of snacks. I thought the owner just wanted a new theme for his business. Serious microbrew lovers were rare in bar owners, a pragmatic lot who relied on distributor special offers and the scent of money. But Melanie said McDavin was a microbrew fan who simply needed some education on the higher profitability of the product. She had sold the owner on a keg of Copper.

Munchies' bar area formed a square in the middle of a large room, allowing customers to approach from all sides. High stools were set up around the bar except for a spot on the far side marked for servers. There, a large copper bar ran from the floor to a foot above the bar top, then arched to the bar where it was fastened. "Servers Only" was burned into the wooden bar top.

Booths circled three of the outside walls of the bar room. The fourth wall showcased a chest level, wide shelf where foods were set out each afternoon. Wall sconces were few but windows let in enough exterior light to make reading the pub menu possible. At night it must have gotten more difficult.

I chose a seat at the bar. The bartender, a clean-cut twenty-nothing, sauntered over and tossed a coaster in front of me. It was close to lunchtime, too early for the snacks.

"Do you have any local beers?" I asked, our standard opening line because the response often indicated both the owner's interest in microbrews and how educated the bartender was to our products.

"We just got the new Barrels seasonal. Oktoberfest."

"Barrels is local?" I asked, reminded of another reason we opened with that request: it measured the strength of our competition.

"They got a brewery over in Skunktown." The bartender waved vaguely toward the city's south end.

"That a lager?"

The bartender shrugged. "They say it is."

"You got anything dark?"

"Let me get you a list." The bartender turned away and I called to his back. "Gimme a Copper." He hesitated, waved acknowledgement and walked to the tap selection.

While the bartender poured my beer, I reviewed the past hour spent with the police. I hadn't given them much to go on with the pickup except the color and that it was a New York license plate. I mentioned the two men in the car, but not the gun. The police hadn't seemed impressed, probably thinking that I had wasted their time.

The bartender interrupted my thoughts, setting the pint of Copper in front of me.

"I'll start a tab." I pushed a credit card across the bar. He took the card, swiped and placed it in a file box by the cash register.

Realizing that I had become an actual suspect had thrown me for a loop. A suspect and now a potential victim.

Shaken, I didn't know what to do. I couldn't go to the brewery in that state and being alone wasn't a good option. I had decided to act like Nate and patronize a bar where we had just opened a new account. I'd work to cement a knob. I needed a beer.

"It's like that tree that falls in a forest: if no one talks about you, do you really exist?"

A group of teachers sat at a table near me. I scanned their table. Two of the group drank light beer, one a soda, and the fourth, the only male, a pint of what looked like Copper. He had spoken.

"What do you teach?" the younger woman, the soda drinker, asked.

"I don't teach anymore," the man said.

"He's an administrator," a light beer drinker explained.

"Don't worry, I'm not here to evaluate you," the man said.

I wondered what they were doing at lunchtime on a school day, then assumed it was a staff training day. The younger woman caused me think of Nate and the women who had passed through his life. After he and Jenna broke up and he'd learned about his cancer, there had been a multitude of them, right up until he was unable to leave home. He used to joke that near the end he had taken advantage of the pity factor. He didn't even have to lie and they'd go home with him. We joked that he'd contracted a different disease, restless penis syndrome.

Still repressing my surging subconscious, I focused on the beer. It was a nice copper color, and clear. Brewed with the Chico yeast strain, it lacked the bitterness of the quintessential pale ale from Sierra Nevada and because of that had gained us a large number of knobs. Despite Melanie's observations that more beer drinkers were drinking IPAs, a lot of people weren't ready for the level of hops that Mo wanted to put in our beer.

I took my first sip. The Copper was fresh, clean, and settling.

Part of the greatness of beer drinking is its immediacy. The freshness of a pint combined with a good environment elevates the moment, pushing the experience past mere enjoyment to thrill. Nate had regularly said that. He likened the immediacy of drinking a good beer to playing a sport. No wonder the two were so connected in the public mind.

The concept of immediacy had been a big change for me. I'd had to shake myself from the philosophical distance I'd developed as a professor. And to the fact that my presence here meant much less to the twenty-nothings than it had to my students. I had to remember that when trying to win over bartenders who could help us.

Many bartenders knew next to nothing about the product: its quality, expense, and the effort that went into each keg. That was a frustration I learned to swallow. Nate had simply bided his time with these guys. The transitional ones never lasted very long and the bartenders that stuck around because they could be trusted by bar owners needed a few positive experiences before they warmed up to our ideas of quality. Sarah often said that they resembled my students and that the best teachers led students to discover things themselves instead of regurgitating information. If bartenders discovered quality on their own, they became our brewery's biggest promoters.

I noticed the Barrels logo on the glass in front of me, and remembered that we needed to reorder glassware. What would Jenna say? Could we afford it? Could we avoid spending money on promotional items?

Paying bills and keeping track of available cash was immediacy, too. Would we become one of the breweries that the mainstream media wrote off lately, taking the slant that microbrewed beer was a fad? Those of us inside the industry knew differently. A decrease in big money investing hadn't reduced the demand for what we produced. For us, navigating a company through this rising demand would determine our success.

Callahans had sufficient capital thanks to Nate, but that made our financial situation no less urgent. We did not want to dip too far into his savings, especially in a time of growth. My brother had pointed to numerous companies that had gone under in the middle of a growth spurt.

"People say I have a great voice," the man at the table was saying. "I love to sing, too, and when my voice is at its alto, I feel good. I know the future."

"Have you ever performed?" the younger woman asked.

"No. I stand on the side of the stage and sing along. Usually I sing better than the people on stage."

"Take a couple ego pills and come back when you wake up," one of the light beer drinkers said.

"Spoken like a true choir girl," the man replied. "I get it. I'm not trying to insult you, just saying that I love to sing but never had the courage to get on stage." I sensed the two of them had met on some stage.

Still avoiding the feelings that could overwhelm me, I ordered a second pint of Copper. Then looked around for a newspaper. The sports section might help me open a conversation with the bartender, the guardian of the knobs. Quality beer or not, sports was an integral part of the daily interaction between bartender and sales person and learning more about it was a good business decision. This also could lead to my asking a bartender what he thought about our beer.

Over time I had refined my conversation to questions about what was going on in the sports of the season rather than playing the fount of knowledge that Nate pulled off so well. Bartenders loved to talk and felt good if they could deliver the latest scores and what they meant to the overall picture.

Seeing no paper, I allowed a tinge of regret to surface. I should have purchased one before coming here.

"I have known three women." The man was speaking and I wondered how long their lunch break would last. "I'm fifty-two and I've known three women. Each took a quarter of my heart. I only have one quarter left and no one's getting that. That quarter dies with me."

"Maybe you could work on giving away a quarter of your beer belly," the light beer drinker said, eliciting a round of laughter.

"This," he pointed to his belly, "is not a beer belly. It's the fuel tank for my love machine."

A gale of laughter followed and I thought again about the immediacy of moments like this. They were addictive. Not in a physical withdrawal type of way, but an addiction that drew you in regularly. The alcohol helped.

"Ready for another?" The bartender stood in front of me and my empty pint glass. The teachers had left.

I didn't realize how quickly I'd drunk the second pint. I looked at my watch. It was still early. On the other hand, I didn't think this bartender was of much influence with the owner, McDavin. For a moment I thought about leaving. Instead, I nodded.

"Same?"

"Could I try a sampler tray of the Barrels beers?" I was pulled in.

21

I was in the parking lot when Melanie arrived. Recognizing that I'd had a few, she helped me into her car.

"Another beer?" I asked, smiling.

"I'm dying for one, but you don't need it. You're tipsy."

"What do you mean?"

"Your voice gets higher when you're drinking. And that smile, it's unmistakable. What were you drinking?"

"Mostly Copper. They also had a bunch of Barrels taps on. I tried them all."

"Wow."

"No, a sampler tray. They still have that house character." I had decided not to mention the pickup truck to anyone before speaking to Sarah, so talk about beer was a welcome diversion.

"I'm not sure how they get away with calling their seasonal a lager," Melanie said.

"There's a lot of that going on."

I fumbled for my wallet and pulled it out, checking to see that I'd remembered my credit card.

"You okay?" Melanie asked.

"No, I mean, I had a trampler say... I mean sampler tray."

Melanie giggled. "I guess you did."

"Thought I'd work on securing a knob."

"You didn't call Sarah to pick you up."

"She's still at work and then has a date," I said.

"I didn't know you had an open relationship."

"We mostly just talk about it."

"You okay?" Melanie asked again. She looked at me closely and for some reason I couldn't explain I started to tear up. It was as if all the issues of the past few days—Nate's death, Stan's accident, our financial mess, the threat, my drunkenness—rushed into my head at one time.

The kiss took me by surprise. Her mouth suddenly found mine, hungry. It reminded me of so many years ago, when in college I'd hook up with women who were bold, daring, yet soft. The open mouth yet insistence that went along with that opening. At the same time, her hand dropped onto my lap.

I jerked away. There was an awkward silence.

"I'm sorry," she said softly.

"I'm married," I mumbled. It sounded stupid.

"No, I'm really sorry," Melanie replied. "That was uncalled for. I don't know what I was thinking."

"It's okay," I said.

"I'll quit," she said.

"No!" I replied, alarmed.

"I feel terrible."

"Don't quit! I need you!" I tried to put my arm around her and she shrugged it off.

"I saw you looking at me a few times," she said. "I thought…" Her voice trailed off.

"I have," I replied. "And I apologize. But I never meant anything."

"I guess I'm used to men wanting that."

"You're a very pretty woman."

"You don't have to soften the blow."

"You are."

"I know. Maybe that's why I seem to attract so many undesirable men."

"You mean like opposites attract?"

She almost smiled, wiped tears on her sleeve and shook her head silently. "I didn't mean to insult you by putting you in that group."

Suddenly thinking more clearly, I could see where this was going. Or at least thought I did. As a university professor, I had slipped out of a few situations over the years and knew the results would fester if not addressed right away. So despite the uncomfortable silence I decided to say something that had been on my mind for some time. After all, it wasn't as if I'd caught her cheating on a test or anything.

"You're the full package, Mel."

"With fragile marked all over it."

"I mean it. You are what any intelligent young man would want."

She smiled. "Accent on the young."

"And you remind me of my brother. "

"Nate?"

"Yes, you remind me of Nate. There. I've said it."

Melanie didn't reply and I continued. "I mean what I say. You have his same self confidence and drive."

"You'd be surprised at what's behind that," Melanie replied.

"And you're a quick study, like him."

She looked at me. "Just don't tell anyone I have Daddy issues."

I laughed to hide my surprise and took her hand. "Nate had a way with words, too. Something you have."

"Thank you."

"I think you have your strengths and weaknesses assessed pretty accurately," I said.

"You know, Mr. Callahan..."

"Ed. Now isn't the time to get formal."

"Ed. You're quite something yourself. This could have gone very differently."

"I guess we'll just have to fantasize," I said.

She laughed again. "Not if we're working together. Anyway, I really have to learn how to control myself around such a buff man."

"Now you're lying to be nice." It was my turn to laugh and it wasn't forced. "The truth is, you scare me."

"What do you mean?"

"I play things pretty safe," I said. "Nate was the risk taker. I'm the cautious one. And it's obvious to me that if we were to have a romantic relationship, I'd be the loser. You may think I'm being nice, but I'm being honest. You are a very impressive woman."

"Good thing you're married."

"Good thing," I repeated.

She was silent for a long moment. Then said, "It's time to get you home."

The next morning I made love with Sarah. Urgently. And she sensed it. "Another tough day?" she asked when we lay on our backs next to each other, my hand locked in hers.

"You could say that. Ending with my own staff trying to seduce me."

"Melanie?"

"Yeah."

"Should I be worried?"

I rolled to my side, put my arms around her and pulled her to me. I began kneading her back. "She's far too young."

"Well... it's not like I'm ignorant of your charms."

"She said something similar."

"I don't know how you got through so many years at the university without bedding some young coed."

"Easy on the compliments," I replied. "My head is already several sizes too large. I mean the adoration of two beautiful women in twenty-four hours!"

"Why not go for the hat trick?" Sarah replied, smiling.

I laughed at that. Long ago I had told her a story about Nate's boast about bedding three women in one day. He'd called it a hat trick.

I had the sex and fidelity thing figured out as far as men were concerned and it had a lot to do with age. When we were young we threw our bodies around, mandated by hormones. The lucky ones avoided unwanted pregnancies. As we aged, our testosterone levels were replaced by fantasies, grasps at what we thought we could accomplish. It's where many men got into trouble, pursuing fantasies as their prowess decreased.

I'd presented my theory to Sarah and she didn't disagree. But she said I'd left out the essential element, focusing on each other's desires. Excluding the clutter, as she called it, in a long term relationship. Inevitable misunderstandings and frustrations led many couples to drift apart. She had often pulled us back from those moments. Or was it I who did that? Perhaps we had learned from each other. Either way, the clutter inherent in any relationship was insignificant when we kept this in mind.

"It's getting late." Sarah began to get up.

"I want to tell you about my visit to the police station."

"Why?"

"Because I need to communicate."

Sarah didn't say anything, turned toward me.

"I think I'm a suspect in Brinkworth's death. And a target."

"That's not good."

I related all that had happened at the precinct and in the car, which I had left at Munchies.

"Now that's something to worry about," Sarah said when I mentioned the gun.

"I wasn't sure they were following me until I took that quick turn."

"No idea who they were?"

I shook my head. "I didn't even mention the gun to the police. I just wasn't sure enough."

"What do you plan to do?"

"Same as I've been doing. Run the brewery. Now more than ever, I'm focused on making it successful. Nate would expect nothing less."

Sarah laid her hand on my chest. "He has an impressive brother."

"I was thinking about Nate and my part in his death. And the dream."

"The burning pond?"

"The swims in a toxic environment. It's what killed him."

"You don't know that. And you certainly didn't know it at the time."

"You've said that to me before. But I should have. Especially just after it rained."

"From what you told me that was when it was the most fun. The water was high and you could go deeper when you dropped off the rope."

"It was also right after Guthman released the worst of their chemical waste."

"You know you never truly grieved for your brother's passing." She stood up and started to rummage through one of her dresser drawers. "Instead, you took Nate's death as a signal to seek revenge against the chemical company you believe killed him. But you never actually grieved.

"People need to grieve," she finished. "Properly."

"I...I..."

"There's no need to answer me. Just think about it. It's something you have to go through in order to move on. I know how much Nate means to all of you at the brewery, but in the end he would want you to move on, to use his memory as an inspiration, not a ball and chain."

Surprised, I looked at her. "I thought we did that."

"Nate told me that. He was a wise younger brother." After an extended silence, Sarah said, "You okay?"

I rolled out of the bed and stood. "I'll keep that in mind. Time to shower."

"I'm first." Smiling, Sarah slipped into the bathroom.

"Together, let's save water."

22

It takes more than one blow to push a person into a desperate act. Furthermore, the distress is difficult to manage, because you cannot focus on—and address—one issue. The blows come in series, building unnoticed but no less powerful. For me, the news that profit had turned to loss was just one among several issues. One moment the brewery was doing great and the next we swam in red ink. We had a trim staff, with everyone working more hours than our payroll indicated. As an owner, I hadn't taken a salary since starting. With a little belt tightening, Sarah's income covered our monthly bills.

Neither Nate nor I had assessed the business beyond that it was growing. It wasn't something either of us spent time learning. Back when Nate and Stan ran Lawn Lords, they never went beyond collecting and spending their earnings and after that we both had simply earned salaries.

We knew the figures: in this industry the first five years were rarely profitable. We also held to the cardinal rule that we would build as our capital allowed. A big expansion would require bank loans, which Nate planned to avoid. This, plus my brother's insistence that we grow without the help of additional partners, left us vulnerable.

Brinkworth's death also shook me. No matter how much we joked about it, or used it to create some publicity, it wasn't an event to celebrate. Someone had died in our building; that would always remain. Police, a suspicious lot by trade, had scoured the brewery, looking in every corner. And Brindisi seemed to have put me in his sights given my past connection to the deceased.

Then there was Stan. The accident hurt us, even with the addition of Melanie to the staff. I had stepped up my game, spending even more time than previously, but all that extra time only revealed how much we left undone. The cause of Stan's accident, no matter how suspicious I found it, was pushed aside given events.

The concerns kept me awake at night more effectively than any issues I had dealt with at the university. Even Sarah's warm body next to me, which usually allowed me to sleep when stressed, didn't help.

Once Sarah had left, I got up and headed to the pool for an early swim. The pool was empty, a quiet, waveless tank of water welcoming me. Swimming usually cleared the cobwebs away, allowing me to focus and seek order to events. This morning it was a mistake.

As I walked from the locker room past the teenagers lolling in the lifeguard chairs, I noticed that one of them wore the sweat pants of my former university. Suddenly I was in the department chair's office on the last day I had ever seen the place. The administration had sent Henry Johnson to order me to get the story of my career spiked. "For Christ's sake, we already have the head stones!" he had said.

I got into the water and started my laps. "Headstones are a good word for them," I had replied, referring to the large granite blocks that bore Arnold Guthman's name and were to be placed in front of the new Chemistry building. A few activist students had announced a plan to decorate them in malformed amphibians taken from the pond where I used to take Nate to swim and fish. No one fished there anymore, but the theatrics of the protest were marvelous. Or so I thought, until they brought the hammer down.

"I don't understand your obsession with this." I clearly remember Johnson's words.

"It's not an obsession," I had replied. "I'm trying to find the truth."

"What is truth?"

"That's a philosophical question. You know as well as I—you've seen the studies—that this is an open and shut case. It's criminal!"

"I know no such thing," Johnson had countered. "Data can be used to prove whatever you want. And I haven't read your studies."

I overlooked this insult to my work. "My data proves he poisoned the pond and water table. He used a treatment system that couldn't remove the toxins, dumping directly into the pond. This needs to be revealed."

"And smear everyone's reputation in the process? Love Canal was 30 years ago!"

"You said that already."

"The dumping wasn't intentional. It's over. People don't want to read about it anymore. Besides, who are you going to go after?"

"The companies responsible, all of them."

"The waste disposal company? Waste Management Services doesn't even exist anymore, so that makes no sense."

"The owners exist, somewhere. And so does the person who supplied them with the waste. They even dumped his waste into the landfill! And you're going to name the Chemistry building after him?" At the time I had refused to ever utter Guthman's name it was so distasteful.

"So what you really want to do is get him in trouble *and* jeopardize our chances to finish this project."

"And you want to sweep it under the rug."

"It's the past! Leave it!"

"Now you're the one who sounds obsessed."

"He worked for the growth of this community! Employed hundreds of people! And you want to blame the guy for making one small mistake?"

"Small mistake?" I had replied, outraged. "You call fauna covered with tumors a small mistake? I saw them with my own eyes! I fished them out of the pond!"

Johnson was silent.

I thought about mentioning the human cost, but without clear scientific connections decided to hold back. "You have the gall to come into *our* community and call this a small mistake!" I had continued. "I'll determine what size the mistake is around here! And you can take this job and shove it!"

At the time I had felt like the local boy who had done well. I wasn't about to cede moral authority to this mealy-mouthed apologist for our community's chemical nightmare. I was the hero. Or so I thought.

But everything is connected, especially the relationships we have with our peers. I had hurt the people around me, most importantly the university administration. I had even managed to alienate those who supported me, stepping out of the ivory tower to ruffle the comfortable nest of our clan. I found myself ostracized.

At the same time, my brother was dying. He had become this bloated, steroid-filled body fighting until the end. He was avoiding hospice with his last bit of energy.

I had only hit lap 20 when the hopelessness swept over me. I had learned so much of this industry, but no longer felt capable of managing Nate's business. Jenna had stopped in again with more devastating numbers. Callahans was definitely losing money. We were buying the basic goods, but our markups were too low, our giveaways too large. We could not sustain this, she said. If I took the time to extrapolate the numbers, I could anticipate a slow decline of Nate's funds and eventual closing of the brewery.

I couldn't see how Barrels, our local competitor, was managing. Their keg prices were even lower, keeping us from raising ours. Wehrmann & Sons had to be taking fifteen to twenty-five percent of each keg, so how did they manage? Did they have a larger, more patient funding source?

Heading toward the deep end, I decided to turn over on my back. I'm not sure why I made the decision; force of habit, I guess, from the training days I'd undergone but abandoned after my years on the school swim team.

"You pushed me." The words popped into my head, a phrase Nate had often used to credit me with making him a better athlete, the high achieving star he had become. What he meant, of course, was that by the older, bigger, more co-ordinated brother including him in games he had been forced to play harder and that made him a better athlete to peers his own age.

Memories of us stripping to our underwear at the pond emerged. Memories of leaping into the water to be the first one to cross "Gunk Strait," past the discharge pipes of Guthman Chemical to the other side. If it was a rainy day, we'd time it so we hit our stride during high flow so we'd be pushed toward the middle of the pond while trying to reach the opposite shore. Coincidentally, at the same time the factory would release its effluent. We reveled in the smell.

Once we reached the opposite shore, we'd congratulate ourselves and laugh. We never stopped to think that there was little aquatic life beyond the occasional fish or amphibians laying on the shore. We were young, strong... and foolish.

An image popped into my head. We were swimming to the tall bank on the other side of the pond. We passed the discharge pipes and reached the tree high up on the bank, where we'd rigged a thick rope that allowed us to swing out into the pond and drop. The Big Rope, we'd called it. After a rainy day we'd stand on the shore and wipe ourselves in slime from the shore, climb the bank, haul the rope back to the wooden guard rail where we could stand. We would then swing out over the pond and let go. The noxious slime we smeared on ourselves would wash off as we dropped into the water. We'd do it until exhausted, then swim back to our side of the pond.

Suddenly, I slammed my head against the cement at the far side of the pool. I had lost my focus. Stunned, I lay in the water on the deep side of the pool. I had lost focus. I couldn't go any longer. Why not just sink to the bottom and let my lungs fill with water? How appropriate a way to deal with everything. My brother was dead, the brewery was crashing, I had failed. First I'd killed him and now I was killing his business.

I sunk, surrounded by the shimmering turquoise tortoise pattern of the pool bottom. I had my weights on, so submerged easily. I couldn't take the last step and let the air escape from my lungs, but it would run out.

I don't know how long it was before I heard a splash and saw a lifeguard swimming furiously toward me. I pushed myself to the surface. There I grabbed the side and coughed, then smiled at the frightened life guard.

"I'll be all right," I told her as my tears hit the water on my face. Can a person cry underwater? I wondered.

23

The letter, written in my brother's familiar script, lay on the kitchen table. Had I missed it when I left for the pool? That seemed impossible. I had drunk my coffee on the run, but the table was in the middle of the kitchen. There were no signs of Sarah having returned, and as far as I knew she had classes all day.

I felt strange, as if something—someone—was reaching out to me from an unseen place. Finally, I picked the letter up.

> Ed,
>
> If you're reading this, you're deep in your own end of the field and there's trouble. I asked Sarah to give

this to you only under those circumstances.

I'm guessing Jenna has already taken over the books, something you and I were never very good at. She's probably already identified and alerted you to the financial problems. That would be Jenna.

Ed, we need a quarterback to move Callahans over the goal line. Quarterbacking came natural to you, reading the defense, ignoring plays sent from the coaches, even changing the call at the last moment to take advantage of what you saw. You decided to leave the game for safer endeavors, but you have what it takes. You're back in charge and should go on the offensive. But you need to do more than play great, you need to lead. I've always known you had that ability, unlike me.

I'm sure you're surprised when I say I lack leadership ability. I'm the brother who won a host of awards, the super-confident class hero. But the fact is, I had serious weaknesses. I worked on my strengths for that very reason. I am just a running back, Ed, the guy who follows a path through the opponent's defense. Most times I don't even realize how the path is forged, all the teamwork behind it. I just run fast and dodge obstacles. But at the end of the game I understand that someone had the conceptual ability to create that path. Someone worked with the team to create the gaps that turned my speed into success. And I always needed a good quarterback. At Callahans, you are that person.

What I never knew was whether you would leave a safe career to enter the challenging world of business. When you said you would, I was thrilled. But I worry about you sticking with it when the game gets tough. I suspected you might lack the confidence to lead from the first time you hesitated, in the first game I ever won against you. It was tennis and you let one of my volleys get past you without trying. You may not remember that moment, but I do. We were young. You still had size and strength over me and should have stepped up to crush me like the bigger brother always does. But you hesitated. You changed your game to fit mine. That's when I knew I had you.

The doubts kept coming. When I first opened the brewery and had the sign made, you told me I had missed the apostrophe. It should have been Callahan's—not Callahans—Brewery. What I knew but didn't say was that there was always more than one Callahan.

The brewery is in trouble. But so you know, this is a common struggle. In this industry every business goes through a rough period in the early stages. The capital I left will get us through, even if it gets a little thin. What is needed is the confidence and skill to guide us down the field.

Quarterbacks get bloodied and you're no exception. In addition to money issues, you've got the Wehrmacht to deal with. They are a relentless machine that would love nothing better than to see Callahans collapse. They are the team to beat, the powerhouse that will crush anyone showing signs of weakness. But they aren't the thugs of yesterday, when distributors could simply off their competition. They do it through the political system, protecting laws that keep their monopolies intact. They will throw everything they have at you, but they are not invincible. They can be beat. The little guy can survive. You and I never saw eye to eye politically, but it's not the political system that's important. It's adaptability to change that matters. This system may be rigged, but it can—it will—change. As the guy at the helm, you are the agent to force that change.

I spent all my energy on the sports field because in the end it showcased competitions with rules. Games played out fairly even if the sides betrayed an astonishing one-sidedness.

The field allowed the little guy to show the guts to take on Goliath.

I left you with a good team. Stan makes a living off sales commissions, lucky to have Jenna putting food on the table. You won't find a more loyal player. Stan and I reigned supreme in school. We went our separate ways after that, but we always talked about opening another business together. When we opened the brewery it was less about us as individual stars than working together as a team. Stan is as strong a player as me, and as quick. He's your tight end. You can go short or long, but you need to point him in the right direction. Do that and he'll score as often as you need him to.

Johnny works his ass off for the chance to make a living wage some day, proud of what we're doing. He's the work horse needed on every successful team. Hard-working and loyal (You'll notice that loyalty is the essential element of every team member), he will sacrifice anything you ask of him. He has always admired what Stan and I created and is selfless in winning. I hired him for that reason, knowing too that he needs constant encouragement and appreciation. He's your running back and when you use him to run a pattern to the end zone, I wouldn't want to be an opponent on the same field.

Jenna brings it all together with her amazing organizational abilities. She's the only woman I ever loved. If that surprises you, given what happened between us, know that as I deal with thoughts of my own mortality, I see that more clearly than ever. Her soft voice, her kindness and generosity, even her hard-headed moments were all things I wish I had appreciated more. It didn't work out between us. I focused too much on the goal, unable to see what I had, and I lost her.

But I left you another team member, a future winner. Junior is my kid, Ed. When Jenna got pregnant, I already knew I wasn't the one for her. She decided to keep the baby and I ran away from the responsibility. Like a good friend, Stan stepped in to support her. And lo and behold, they fell in love. When Jenna experienced Stan's love as compared to my ambivalence, she chose the better path for her and for Junior. I knew he would do a better job raising a son than I. And that Jenna would be better off. I wasn't the guy for her.

Truth be told, I envy you and Stan. You always spoke about the excitement of my single life, but your relationship with Sarah and Stan's with Jenna were more enviable. I think you two appreciate the fairer sex and will experience far happier lives than I would ever have known.

I put a lot of thought into this letter. About what makes you and me different. It's that difference that makes us great, Ed. You often told me you would spend nine lives trying to live up to my performance level. The secret is that I felt the same. I wanted what you had, a lifelong mate, a job that paid the bills yet left time for leisure, and a touch of activism, a moral compass. But this was the industry I chose.

There are an incredible number of great people in the brewing world, beginning with our staff. Remember that. Having worked in several other industries, I'm telling you, there is no comparison.

So to the quarterback, the guy who inspired me to achieve, it's time to play. I leave this world thinking you will take Callahans to new heights. The goal line may seem a long way off, but you're the leader needed to get us there. It's what you were always good at. You have the brains and are a playmaker. It's time to switch on the Ed I was lucky enough to grow up with, the guy who could turn on his game with the cool calculatedness of a winner.

And now you know you're helping to continue a legacy that has a de-

scendant. Keep the link between generations strong. Be the leader. I know
you have it in you.

I will love you always,
your brother Nate

I set the letter on the table, remained seated, unable to move.

24

I arrived for Mo's beer tasting by late morning. The door was tightly sealed and the street light fixed. Our van was outside, parked next to Mo's car. No ladder outside the building indicated that Johnny had finished the skylight trim. I entered the building and stopped, wowed by the sunlight playing on the open floor where Brinkworth had fallen. Or been pushed. The skylight frame glowed with a new coat of varnish.

Johnny and Melanie were in the office listening to Mo tell a story, this one about his great-grandfather Barley Charley. With Mel in the house, Mo had a fresh set of ears.

I'd heard the story: Barley Charley lived during Prohibition and for anyone who cared to do the math, his age just about fit.

"How did he get caught up in bootlegging?" Melanie asked, acknowledging my entrance with a smile and a nod.

"He started as a bathtub brewer." Mo arranged the taster glasses on his desk in sets of four. "He wasn't a great one. In those days it was more about making an alcoholic beverage than an award winning beer. Like Canada, where home brewing is more about avoiding government taxes than making great beer. He decided to deliver his brews and earn some extra money. He was also a big FDR fan, one of those patriots who believed that Americans needed a drink.

"The brewing went well; it was distribution that got him in trouble. The bootleggers who controlled the black market were not happy. Barley wasn't the brightest star in the sky, if only for thinking that if he stuck to beer they would leave him alone."

"The Wehrmacht," Johnny added, caught up in the story.

"Right," Mo said. "Descendants of the very same."

"I've heard a little of the family history from George," Melanie said.

"Who's George?" Johnny asked.

"The brother of the guy you hit at Benson's, a Wehrmann," Mo said. "Anyway, Barley Charley refused to stop delivering beer. So they fitted him with a pair of cement boots and dropped him in the river."

"And?" Johnny asked, keeping the story going.

"He sunk to the bottom... and started walking. Slowly, over wrecks, piles of garbage, through the mud, holding his breath until he reached shore."

"That's not the story!" Johnny said, looking triumphant at having caught Mo in a discrepancy. "You said he grabbed the anchor rope from a fishing boat and pulled himself to the surface."

"He's right," I added.

"The story changes every time you tell it!"

Mo shrugged. "Gotta keep it interesting."

"I like the image better," Melanie said. "What happened next?"

"They hired him," Johnny interjected. "Or is that part different?"

"No, you got that right, Flex," Mo said, unperturbed. "Barley Charley walked into their warehouse, sat down and said that if they cut off the boots, he would deliver their beer, too. He agreed to a cut and they hired him on the spot. Told him he had to open new markets for his product. They agreed, their final offer."

"The final offer," I repeated. If you wanted to stay in the business during that time, you worked for the Wehrmacht. They were well known for making a final offer.

Mo examined me. "You look like hell. Your Check Liver light click on last night?"

"I feel great," I replied. "Ready to sell some beer."

"Dead Lawyer is a hit," Melanie said. "When will the next batch be ready?"

Mo put down his glass. "Damn girl, you have some learning to do. Lesson number one, don't let the boss steer you back to work-related topics."

"Roof repair looks great," I said.

"All sealed and ready for another lawyer," Johnny said.

"Please, no more lawyers," I replied.

"How about a cop?" Mo suggested. "Oh yeah, that reminds me, the guy from the precinct called. What's his name...?"

"Brindisi."

"That's the one. He left a phone number. It's on your desk."

"Excuse me for a moment." I retrieved the number and left the office.

"Brindisi."

"Hello Officer. This is Ed Callahan, returning your call."

"Mr. Callahan, thank you for calling back. I just wanted to inform you that we are closing the Brinkworth case. The man's alcohol was pretty high and we've concluded that he fell. No fault of yours or the business. We're not sure what he was doing on your roof, but it appears that it was an accidental death."

"Thank you," was all I could manage.

"You're welcome. Have a good day."

I closed my phone, stunned. Once again I noticed the lights playing on the floor. My mind sought a distraction. It had been an astute move to open up part of the roof to light. Before that the building had been dark, with electrical work that needed updating. With natural light, Nate had reduced the need and expense of new wiring and lights.

"Ed!" The call came from the office. I entered and Mo was finishing pouring some Copper from a pitcher. "Are we ready for the morning prayer? Melanie needs to learn it."

"You're right," I agreed. "You want to lead?"

We each picked up a glass and Mo began.

"Our lager, which art in barrels, hallowed be thy grain.

"I will drink, at home and in the brewhouse.

"Give us this day our foamy head,

"And forgive us our drunkenness as we forgive those too drunk to bless us."

We lifted our glasses and drank. Then Mo continued.

"Lead us not to incarceration, and deliver us from hang-overs.

"For thine is the beer—the ale and the lager."

"Barmen!" we all said.

I finished my sample. "Speaking of beer, I'd like to ask Mel to give us an idea of what's been selling lately."

"IPAs," Mel said immediately. "They're taking over the taps."

"Who's drinking them?" Mo asked.

"Everyone."

"Even women?"

"They're coming around."

"Time was when you couldn't get a bitter beer near Sarah," I said. "Now she loves a good IPA. At the same time she'll tell you she doesn't like bitter beer."

"It's all in the flavor," Mo said. "The IPAs of today have more than just bitterness, they have flavor."

"So when you gonna do something about that, brewer man?" Johnny asked.

"Drink something besides Copper and you'd see that I already have," Mo replied. "Our IPA has a lot more flavor than when I first brewed it. A veritable fruit bowl. And now we also have Dead Lawyer."

"Sam just ordered one," Melanie said.

"Whoa!" Mo said. "Mister Malt?"

"He's finally coming over to the hop side. Customer demand."

"Anything else you notice?" I asked.

She thought a few moments, then said, "The diversity of styles—traditional and new—is growing. That plays into Mo's new ideas."

"Just keep it within reason," I cautioned. Mo's creativity and his almost unnatural ability to foresee trends in consumer preference had a down side. More than once he had introduced a new flavor years before bars were ready for it. It was the constant battle of pushing the envelope versus producing something bar owners were willing to buy and consumers to drink.

Mo pulled a bottle out of the refrigerator. "Try this and let me know what you think."

"Aroma first," Mo said, once we all had a glass in our hands.

I sniffed the beer. "Nice, but I don't recognize the hop."

"Number 247, experimental," Mo said. "Got a touch of charcoal. Do you get that?"

"I don't have the nose you do, but I think you nailed the aroma."

I swirled the beer again, then smelled. "I do get a charcoal-like note. Might be the power of suggestion."

"I think it's there," Mo said.

"Name," I said. Since taking over, I had stressed the importance of names. Whole breweries had been built on a good name. The big guys knew this and were in constant search for something new, whether it was ice, dry, or a powder mix tossed into their beer. But the name mattered. While the principal difference between the micros and the penguins was flavor, a brand with a catchy name—which everyone sought—was undeniably part of the path to financial success.

"Not sure how it'll go over on the market but if Dead Lawyer sticks, we can build on that," Mo said.

"How about Burned Lawyer," Johnny suggested.

"I'm thinking a series of Lawyer beers," Mo replied.

"What about Prosecutor as a doppelbock?" Johnny suggested.

"We'll need a Defendant," Melanie added.

"I'm guessing The Judge would be our barley wine," I said.

"Good, Nate... I mean Ed." Mo had mistakenly called me by my brother's name more than once and I'd gotten used to it, in fact felt flattered. One of the family.

25

My well-being didn't last long. Our family was together and the business healthy, but I couldn't dismiss the events of the past few weeks. I was missing something.

I had been too shocked to ask Brindisi if any progress had been made on Stan's accident. Did it even matter anymore? Was Nate correct, that Prohibition-era tactics were a thing of the past? Was my thinking too conspiratorial? Still the broken turn signal bothered me. The police had dismissed that incident as an accident as well. Beyond thinking he'd been bumped, Stan hadn't shed much light on his going off the road. What did it mean? Was I presuming too much, as Sarah thought? I usually found her conclusions accurate, but perhaps I hadn't sufficiently explained the situation.

Then there was the shotgun. Had I actually seen it? Had I been followed? Tracking down the pickup seemed logical, but that was a police task and they had closed the investigation. Was there even a connection between Brinkworth's death and the pickup? Given the comments I'd heard at the station about the dead man, were the police hiding something?

Lastly, were the two incidents connected? Brinkworth's brewery death had occurred in the brewery. I felt sure—an instinct, really—that I was missing a key piece of the puzzle and that it was staring me in the face.

Sarah left town that week. It was spring vacation for her students and she wanted to spend the time with her younger sister, who had just gone through a difficult divorce. I decided not to go. We had a heavy production schedule and everyone was needed. I also was not ready to discuss my suspicions with her until I had more to go on.

The decision to revisit the Wehrmann delivery truck yard came from Melanie. I was finishing a conversation with Biers when she returned from a sales call. She waited until I was off the phone.

"I was thinking about that signal light."

"What were you thinking?" I asked, surprised.

"All the trucks are in by five. We could visit after that. And before five in the morning; George always boasted that they made their millions between five and five and that left him half his life to party."

"Do you have a plan?"

"Nothing beyond that."

"So we visit the yard at midnight. Find the truck. And..."

"Maybe it's nothing..." she began.

"I'm willing," I interrupted. "Tonight?"

She nodded.

"Do you have black clothes?" I asked, trying to think like a burglar.

She laughed, "Does a woman have black clothes? Ed, open your eyes. We all wear black. Often."

"When I'm looking at women, I'm not looking at the clothes," I shot back.

"Very clever."

That night was perfect for breaking and entering I remember thinking as we walked through a wooded area next to the warehouse. A cloud-covered sky and no rain gave us good cover. The ten foot high fence surrounding the delivery trucks had barbed wire running along its top, so we started by searching its entire circumference. At the far side, near the gate into the fenced area, against the building, the end post stood inches from the building.

"Here!" Mel whispered. She was dressed from head to toe in black. "I can squeeze through."

As she slipped through the small space between the fence pole and building I couldn't help but think of the numerous spy movies I'd watched. Except this was real. And probably foolish.

It was obvious that I wouldn't fit through the opening.

"I can go over the top."

"How are you going to reach it?"

"I'll get the keg dolly from the van. Lean it against the fence and climb up."

"Too dangerous. Give me the piece and I'll look," Mel suggested, a better idea for a pair of amateur sleuths.

I pushed the broken piece and a pen light through the narrow opening. "It's one of the mid-sized trucks," I said, remembering the one I'd seen at Sam's bar.

While Melanie searched for the truck, I scanned the top of the building. There were cameras mounted along the roof edge, but I doubted they had infrared capability if they even operated at night. Nonetheless, wearing black clothes had been a good idea.

It seemed that Melanie was gone forever and doing nothing for that long made me as impatient as I'd ever felt. I scanned the building again, looking for camera motion. Nothing. I reconsidered scaling the fence, but the thought of the barbed wire ripping my clothes or skin kept me from attempting it. One of us in the truck yard was sufficient. Besides, if someone spotted us, she could slip out easily, leaving me inside, trapped.

Despite my fidgety impatience, Melanie returned without incident. "I found a match!" she whispered triumphantly. "I have the make and model and license plate number."

"Good work." I wondered why we were whispering; the area appeared to be deserted. Our original fear that we would encounter guard dogs appeared unfounded.

Once back at the van, Melanie held out a small plastic bag of white powder. ""I have something else. Cocaine."

"What...wh...where did you find that?"

"In the truck with the broken light."

"How..."

"I knew where to look. George once told me he'd found a stash under the bottom side of the seat of a truck, that that was where Tony stored his drugs." I didn't reply and she continued. "He claimed his brother started every day by snorting the stuff. Called it white coffee. He often complained that Tony was snorting the family profits up his nose."

"So you think he might have been coked up that morning, and rammed Stan?"

"The thought occurred to me."

"What would Tony be doing driving a delivery truck?"

"He liked to drive. That was well known around the office."

"What are we going to do with the cocaine?"

"I don't know yet, I just grabbed it. But I have an idea."

"Which is..." I encouraged.

"I know someone in the front office. He does the delivery schedules."

Thinking quickly, I extrapolated. "So we see who was driving the truck on the morning in question."

"Right."

"And then..."

"Not sure."

"Let the chips fall where they may," I said, not wanting to discourage her. "Let's get out of here." My immediate concern was having drugs in the van this late at night. I could see the headline: *Brewery Owner Arrested at 3 a.m. Found with Cocaine and Young Female Employee.* Even Mo couldn't come up with a marketable beer name for that.

We arrived at Melanie's apartment. "Want to come up for tea? I promise not to seduce you."

I smiled. "Sure. We should probably decide what to do, if anything, with that." I pointed to the bag of powder on the seat.

"I'll keep it," she said.

Melanie's apartment was small, sparsely decorated, but neat. The foyer led into a living room, the largest room in the place. A large couch and two straight-back chairs with a matching pattern and wood arms surrounded a worn Oriental rug. On each side of the couch, separating it from the chairs, were carved wooden end tables. A small television sat on a cabinet across from the couch, giving the room the look of furniture passed down from grandparents. Above the television a photo of Melanie with an older man took front stage. Both were dressed in bright red racing coveralls and standing next to a car that must have been modified for racing. Her father, I thought.

To the left a kitchen extended out to a small dining area and a second entrance back into the living room. To the right was a bathroom door, then beyond that one that led to a bedroom. "Nice and homey," I commented.

"Not much room for guests," Melanie said. "When visitors come, I have the pullout. Have a seat, I'll heat some water. Bathroom is over there."

The bathroom was in blue down to the bar of soap. I lifted the seat and urinated, made sure to set it back down after flushing. I hadn't expected pink, but strict blue seemed overwrought.

"What do you think we should do with it?" I asked, once we had settled onto the couch.

"What about your police connection?"

"Brindisi? It'd be quite a stretch explaining what to us seems like a logical series of events."

"Would it push him to re-examine the case?"

"I'm not sure there even is a case. I think it's just a report on the accident. Besides, if we tell him, he's going to ask how we found the cocaine. I doubt our illegal, late night excursion will impress him."

"Let's put it back, then tell him."

"Planting evidence," I said, playing the role of the officer.

"Re-planting. It was already there."

"And how do we explain that we know it's there?"

"How about telling him that we know that's where Tony kept it. I can say I worked there and heard the rumors." I could see she doubted the strategy, even as she defended it.

I sipped my tea. "English Breakfast?"

"Irish."

"Unable to tell the difference. Not British enough, I guess."

Melanie set her tea down suddenly. "I'm thinking of asking Johnny out."

"A date?"

She nodded. I was silent.

"You don't approve?"

"Why does that matter?"

"You're my boss. We both work at the brewery."

"When it comes to dating, I don't make judgments," I said. "You'll find out soon enough if it was a smart move. Or maybe it will take years."

"I don't want to complicate the atmosphere."

"Johnny's a good kid. So are you. But I've been living with and loving the same woman for over ten years. With not a lot of experience before that. I'm not sure I'm the one to give you advice."

"I value your opinion," Melanie said. "You've got a natural approach and good instincts."

"Well, work and love are two different things. With Johnny I'd say try to make it look like he asked you out. He's quite traditional. I do know he likes you a lot." I finished my tea. "I should go. Early day tomorrow."

"Our lesson on hops."

"I'm looking forward to it," I said.

I thanked her and headed home, leaving the bag of cocaine on her kitchen counter.

26

"Mmmm... hops!" Mo lifted the pellets to his nose and smelled deeply. Then held his hand out to Mel. She breathed in the aroma, closing her eyes. I did the same, taking several of the green pellets from Mo's hand and crumbling them. The slightly sticky substance gave off a resinous pine aroma.

"The hops plant is dioecious," Mo began.

"Meaning?"

"Males and females are separate plants. Brewers use only the female, the flower. The resins she produces, what are normally used to trap the male pollen, contain the oils we need for beer. The male plants are kept away to avoid fertilization and seeds."

"Like pot," I said.

"Correct. Same Family, Cannabaceae, without the hallucinogenic effect." Mo dropped the hop pellets into a bucket, which he picked up and dumped into the brew kettle. "These are Centennial hops," he said.

"Is that where you're going with Dead Lawyer?" I asked.

Mo nodded. "Pure West Coast. They got too many lawyers.

"Traditionally, hops were used to add bitterness to beer, to balance the sweetness of the malt," he continued.

"And to preserve it," Melanie added.

"Very good. I can see you've studied." As he spoke, the aromas of the hops Mo had thrown into the kettle wafted toward us, a delicious piney bouquet that overwhelmed the cereal-like malt smell lingering from earlier in the brew.

"So we add these hops early, for bitterness," Mo continued. "The boiling wort emulsifies the acids, which give us the bitterness to balance the sweetness of the malt."

"You said something about freshness," Mel said.

"Freshness is king," Mo said. "Especially with hops. But that's most important with the later additions, which we'll get to. For now, we watch to make sure there's no boil-over. Wouldn't want to lose any of that bitterness."

Mel and I descended from the brewing platform while Mo remained, intent upon the boil.

"I got a look at the drive schedule," Mel said.

"What schedule?" I asked, puzzled at first.

"The delivery truck schedule. On the day of the accident."

"What did you find out?"

"He was driving the delivery truck."

"Tony Wehrmann?"

She nodded.

"How did you find out?"

"The guy who does the scheduling at Wehrmann. He had a crush on me that I played on. Also knows all the inside dirt."

I remained silent, letting her talk.

"Said he remembered that day well because not only did our friend return the truck late that morning, he reported a dented front end and broken light. Said he'd hit a guard rail."

"Sounds like a solid lead."

"Also said he looked a little hyped up that morning."

"Was this a regular route?"

"Apparently he does the early morning drop-offs."

"So he must have passed Stan on his route more than once."

"They even had words. Stan actually reworked his schedule to avoid arriving at the same bars together. Bottom line, he knew the route."

"Tony?"

Again, she nodded. "Something else I found out. He used to work for a disposal company."

I noticed that she had yet to say Tony's name. "Waste Management Services, no longer in business."

"I'm surprised I never saw him in court." I said, remembering the name and the line of people Brinkworth had subpoenaed to make his case to close the Sand Ridge landfill.

"I guess it was a big secret, at least that's what my guy said. Also made me promise not to reveal where I got the information."

"We have a rolling boil," Mo said, descending from the brew platform. He adjusted the lever that sent heat to the brew kettle. Then turned to us. "History of hops, 101.

"The plant was first used in beer in central Europe, what is now Germany, land of beer drinkers. As its use grew, the hop plant became more prevalent, pushing out other plants as a natural preservative. Even the British began to use it instead of more traditional ingredients like heather and wormwood."

"And America?" Melanie asked.

"Interesting story," Mo said. "The original settlers of New England landed where they did, Plymouth Rock, because they had run out of beer." He met our look of disbelief with a shrug. "Look it up, it's in the ship's diary."

"Which ship?" Melanie asked.

"The Mayflower, of course. Anyway, Americans began cultivating the hop soon after landing. Both British and Dutch settlers drank beer and needed the ingredients. Growing it is somewhat simple as hops are started from replanting root stock. And they grow fast, like weeds."

"Anywhere?" I asked.

"Hops grow best between the 35th and 55th degrees of latitude. Climate is everything."

"Meaning New England," I said.

"Very good. In fact, New England and New York were our principal providers until Prohibition. After that failed experiment, hop growing moved to the Northwest.

"Speaking of which, it's time to add more hops. Follow me." Mo headed toward the cooler and we followed. Inside the cooler, he pointed to a long metal shelf. "Those are boxes of hops. Have to keep them cold and vacuum packed. Oxygen is the enemy, gives beer that cardboard taste you get from old beer."

"Freshness," Melanie said.

"You got it." Mo picked up a bucket of hop pellets that Johnny had prepared for him. It was full to the brim. "Had to convince Flex to up the level for Dead Lawyer." He smiled and I saw why Mo had earned the reputation as a hop fanatic. The amount seemed excessive even to me. "These are for flavor and aroma."

We left the cooler and ascended the brewing platform. Mo dumped the contents of the bucket into the kettle. "We cut the boil and let these beauties stew in the hot wort. We don't want to emulsify the acids, instead we are aiming for pure hop flavor."

He turned to us. "U.S. brewers have started doing more late addition hops, giving beer more flavor. Changing the beer world for the better, one pellet at a time."

"The flavor is what I love," Melanie said.

"Interestingly, that's one of the things that has turned women on to beer," Mo replied, turning to Melanie. "Traditionally, they have disliked bitterness. As the gatherers in ancient clans, women have an innate avoidance for bitter plants, which indicate poison. But with the addition of flavor in hops, they have began to drink more IPAs."

"There he goes again," Johnny said, interrupting the lesson. "The world according to hoodwink."

"Admittedly a theory of mine," Mo conceded.

"How many tons for the dry hop?"

"Same as last time," Mo said. "But let's wait on that, want to get them fresh out of the package."

"You keeping an eye on this guy?" Johnny asked me. "I'm betting the cost of this beer will top any he's made yet."

"Some beers are going to be expensive," Mo retorted. "But as you can see, the people love India Pale Ales, especially my latest."

"It's the name," Johnny said.

"Where does the India come in?" I asked.

Mo started to reply, then turned to Melanie. "This one's yours."

"British colonialism. The English breweries had to ship beer to India, a colony at the time, and that meant a long voyage around Africa. So they added extra hops to the pale ales they were brewing at the time, to preserve the beer for the voyage. More hops, longer lasting beer, India Pale Ale."

"Very good," Mo said. "There were some benefits to British imperialism."

"I wasn't overly impressed with the India Pale Ales across the pond," I said.

"No, as I said, American brewers are taking the style to new heights. I predict the English will follow."

The office phone rang. I noticed the time, after nine. Melanie beat me to it. I waited next to her while she took an order. She hung up, smiled and gave me a thumbs up. "We just got a knob at The Horned Toad!"

"Nice work."

"He wants it right away, says he's got a spot he needs to fill."

"Time to visit and pour the cement," I replied. "Tonight?"

27

"So tell me professor, why are beer distributorships so powerful?" Melanie had taken to calling me professor, a title my students had loved to use in our classroom give and takes.

We sat in The Horned Toad, an English-themed pub owned by Dan Hutchinson. Melanie capturing a knob here was no easy task given the bar owner's desire to showcase English beers. In Hutchinson's case, this meant beers like Bass, John Courage, Newcastle Brown, and if adventurous, Double Diamond or bottles of Whitbread. The occasional knob of Sierra Nevada Pale Ale or a Barrels product popped up, but U.S. beers were rare in British themed bars.

The Horned Toad was a new build, but the owners had done what they could to make it look worn and distinct. It was one of the better attempts to fashion a bar similar to ones I had visited in England. Long bar, booths along the wall, tables that could be removed, if needed, for large crowds.

Dan Hutchinson was a former athlete who had returned home to build a business. He had played ball with Nate. Melanie had leveraged that friendship into an agreement to try our beer. She had approached Hutchinson with our Copper, the easiest—and the most English—of our beers. Nate had modeled Copper after an English Pale Ale, hoping to ride on the coat tails of the success of import beers, which had been selling increasingly well for the past decade.

"Distributors." I picked up my beer. "Tell me when I get too pedantic."

"Have I ever not told you?" Melanie replied, smiling.

"No. You were good at that. For which I thank you." I drank, then set my beer down. "Historically, beer distributors were small, family-run businesses who dealt with much larger, more powerful breweries. As such, the laws governing the trade—and given that after Prohibition the alcohol trade was highly regulated—protected small businesses. No one wanted another elephant in the room, a brewery in this case, to act so ruthlessly that it could send the businesses distributing their product into bankruptcy.

"In the past, this was a sensible approach. Distributorships carved up territories, taking responsibility to deliver beer to the retail outlets there. Breweries focused on supplying the product. And retailers sold beer to the public. This is the essence of the three tier system, keeping the tiers separate financially."

"What we see today," Melanie observed.

"Different," I said. "What we see today are brewery-restaurants producing beer and selling it. In many states we also see operations like ours that distribute their own beer. The changes required legal modifications, which vary widely in each state."

"Why did Nate choose to distribute Callahans beer rather than use a distributor?"

"A couple reasons. First, we are still small. Second, the entire scenario has been turned on its head. We now have small breweries popping up around us, but as more of them open distributorships are merging, or closing. The small family outlets are growing larger. And depending in large part on their cash cows, the national brands."

"The Bud/Miller/Coors."

"Correct," I said. "The national brewing concerns carried distributorships to a bigger level, and expect those businesses to focus on their brands. That's where the money is. Small breweries like ours have little to no influence over them. Despite the massive investment and work load, Nate always cherished our independence. In New York, we're allowed to distribute our own beer so he chose that model."

We sat quietly, absorbing the noises of a bar slowly filling with patrons.

"Do you plan to ever give up the distribution side?" Melanie asked.

"We'd have to if we went out of state," I replied. "Or grew so large that we needed help covering the south. Or the city."

"New York City?"

I nodded.

"A lot of beer drinkers there."

"And it's locked up by the distributors, at least for the time being." I drank. "Anyway, that's a decision we can kick down the road. I'd love to see small, independent distributors open, ones that would focus on microbrews, but the capital investment is enormous. Warehousing, trucks, labor..." I trailed off as I noticed Hutchinson approaching.

Dan Hutchinson had a reputation as a bar owner who worked the industry mercilessly. Signage—especially neons—were a requisite as were discounts, meaning all the freebies he could get. Since he did a good business, distributors usually gave him what he wanted. Or maybe it was just that he was more demanding. Which is what surprised me when Melanie said she'd gotten him to take our beer with no special deals involved.

She stood and reached out to shake his hand. After introducing us, she complimented him on the place, pointing out the booth design and wall posters as bringing authenticity to his business.

"Thank you," Hutchinson said, then turned to me. "I hear you run Callahans now."

"I do."

I half expected him to begin working me for a deal. Instead, he simply said, "Thanks for coming in. I know you must be busy, but it means a lot to see you here."

"It's my pleasure," I said. "I like to get out of the back office to meet our customers." I left unsaid the obvious, that bar owners were big on meeting the brewery owners.

"How long have you been in charge?" Hutchinson asked.

"Not long, a year. I took it over when Nate died."

"That took us by surprise," Hutchinson said. "The guy seemed invincible."

Melanie came to the rescue while I fought back a sudden rush of emotion. "Nate had a great vision for the brewery. Said he wanted to make fresh, drinkable, locally produced beers."

Hutchinson looked around him, then pointed toward the bar where pints of beer mingled with a lesser number of bottled, mainstream offerings. "People seem to like it."

"Do you need anything to help promote the beer?" I asked, recovered.

"I think we're fine. The posters help."

"I wondered if you would be interested in a Coming Out party," Melanie said. Then began to explain what that entailed. I excused myself, heading to the rest room while Melanie worked her magic. I was always amazed at how well she spoke for a person her age.

Hutchinson had departed by the time I returned, and Mel and I sat drinking our beers slowly.

"I like this place," I observed. "No music and muted televisions allow for the noise of people talking, the crack of good conversation."

"It's relaxing."

"A good place to drop the inhibitions of the work day, and so begin the social milieu amidst the scent of good beer."

"Poetic," Mel replied. Two beers appeared. "I ordered for you."

"Thank you."

"I've decided not to date Johnny," she said suddenly.

"Why not?"

"I don't want to complicate things."

I nodded. "I'm surprised. You're usually very decisive."

"I told you because I wanted your opinion. I hadn't really made up my mind yet."

"It's probably wise to avoid romance with someone you work with closely every day."

"He's pretty intense," Melanie replied. "And I'm not sure I'm ready to date again."

"How long has it been?" I asked.

I wasn't expecting what happened next. Melanie's upper lip quivered slightly and her face clouded. She reached for a bar napkin, wiping her eyes.

"I'm sorry," I said. "I didn't mean..."

"Not your fault," she said. "It's been two years. Since George."

"It hurt that much?"

She didn't respond, her face stoning over.

"I don't mean to pry," I said quickly. "That whole thing with George. I didn't mean..."

"It wasn't George," she interrupted. "It was Tony. He raped me."

"I'm sorry," was all I could managed, stunned.

"And George did nothing." Her voice was even, expression deadpan.

"I can see why you're reluctant to date again."

"It was at a party. We were drinking. I was on my way out, actually, leaving because George was flirting again. I decided to leave and went upstairs to get my coat. He trapped me."

"Are you okay talking about it?" I looked around, concerned about being overheard by other patrons.

"You're easy to talk to," Melanie replied. At the same time she moved away from me. "He told me he'd put all the coats in one room and offered to show me. I didn't suspect a thing. When we got there he asked for a brotherly hug. I was a little drunk, didn't see it coming. Next thing I knew his hands were all over me. I told him no but he kept saying it was for his brother. I tried fighting but he was like steel and only seemed to get more excited as I resisted. He threatened to hurt me. So I let him. I didn't fight."

"He's strong. I'm not sure fighting would have helped."

Melanie didn't say anything, sat emotionless.

I sat quietly, unable to come up with anything empathetic.

"I've never told a man before," she finally said.

"You didn't report it?"

She shook her head. "I told George. When he found out he screamed at me, accused me of seducing his brother. He was always jealous, but this... he said he never wanted to see me again." We sat in silence for a while. Then, Mel added, "Turns out he was known for that. I went to a rape survivors group for a while and his name came up more than once."

"Tony?" Even saying his name was distasteful.

Melanie nodded. "A serial rapist." Then, "I hate those bastards."

28

That night I called Sarah. It was late but she answered.

"How's your sister?"

"Still very sad."

"I miss you."

"I miss you, too. How's the brewery?"

"Going well. The Dead Lawyer outline has proven a hit. People want to stand on it with their beer and get their photo taken. Especially lawyers."

"Maybe you should set up a photo station and charge money."

"Good idea. I'll add it to my list." I laughed. "Meanwhile, we're scrambling to keep up with supply. That's all people want to drink now."

"I'm sure Mo has that covered. Speaking of whom, did your brew lesson go well?"

"Yes, very educational. Learning this part of the business will help. I'm glad Mo suggested it. And of course, he's as funny as ever. Would have made a good teacher."

"And your investigation?"

"I've learned a lot more, just can't seem to piece it together."

"What have you learned?"

"Mel and I visited the Wehrmann truck yard."

"You cheating on me again?"

"Of course. Cat's away."

"You naughty little mouse, you."

"No worries, it's just a fling."

"You sure? I know all about the male's attraction to the younger of his species."

"I thought we agreed that it's okay as long as we keep to the same species."

"And I'm growing old," Sarah mused.

"Well, there's that little wrinkle to the right of your left eye. It'll grow and..."

"Careful." She cut me off.

"Hey, I like wrinkles. Look at all mine."

"Just save some for me," Sarah said.

"I can't wait to get your naked ass into bed."

"That's more like it." She laughed. "And it's only been three days."

"I miss you," I repeated.

"So what did you find in the truck yard?"

I told her about the delivery truck and broken signal light match, and the cocaine. I also told her what Melanie said about the truck and Tony Wehrmann driving, finishing with his connection to the waste disposal company.

"It sounds like the pieces *are* starting to fit," Sarah said.

"I think they do, I just don't know where to begin. The police wrote this off as an accident. When I pointed out the light and dent, they kept repeating how lucky Stan was to have hit the embankment, that he hadn't gone over the cliff."

"What about the pickup?"

"Dead end. With only a color, make and model, the police won't go any further. They say nothing happened that they can do anything about." I changed subjects. "Tell me more about your week. Have you been doing anything interesting?"

"We visited a glass museum today. I found it interesting but Cindy didn't last long. She started crying, said even the appreciation of art raised emotions she wasn't ready to deal with."

"The breakup was quite abrupt. As far as I knew everything was fine between her and Sam."

"How often that happens."

"She's lucky to have a sister like you."

"I have a good teacher."

"What do you mean?"

"Empathy. You're the king of it. It's why I decided that you were marriage material."

"Tell me more," I replied, surprised by the turn in the conversation.

"I remember the very day I decided. I told you my mother was dying and you offered to drive me to her home. Then stuck by me when most men would have disappeared. You took care of me, loved me even more."

"It seemed natural. You were taking it hard."

"Your empathy and care meant everything to me."

"I hate to think that your mom's early passing was my good fortune," I said. "I know how much she meant to you."

"It's not just that. It revealed something about you, that you were a good, dependable man. The rest is secondary. I just try to keep it fun."

"It still is."

"You probably don't remember, but that was about the time I started pushing for something longer term."

"I never put the two together. And I never thought supporting you was anything but a show of love."

"It meant everything," Sarah repeated.

"It's funny how as close as we are, I'm still learning things about you."

"And about others," Sarah said.

We didn't talk for a while, then I asked, "How long have you known about Junior?" I had shown Sarah the letter before she left for her sister's.

"Not long after he was born."

"How could I have missed that?"

"One of the other things I love about you is your ivory tower intellectualism. It so steeps you in higher level thoughts that you miss the obvious. While sometimes frustrating, it's also amusing at times."

"Well put," I said. "And something I need to hear after the tongue-lashing Jenna gave me today for neglecting our tax filings. Some things should not be overlooked."

"How is she doing with that?"

"Great. Mo calls her the dollar cop, always interrogating him on his expenditures."

"That's a good thing."

"It is. It's something neither Nate nor I did very well."

"What about the taxes?"

"Says she has it squared away. I don't know how she does it all, Callahans books, her job, the baby."

"She has Stan."

"He plans to return soon."

"They'll find a way. You have a good crew, Ed. Your brother always said that."

"They keep Callahans strong," I replied.

"What Nate never mentioned was your empathy."

"Not in his character."

"I know, but it's one of the key ingredients in keeping the business successful. It's what motivates people. You may not see it, but your mentoring for Melanie means the world to her. You've created an unbreakable loyalty."

"I learned something about Melanie tonight." I told her about the rape.

"Poor girl," Sarah said.

"She never reported it. I'm not sure that was the best decision, but I do know bottling it up has affected her for the worse."

"It sounds like she did open, to you. She's lucky to have you."

"Just trying to keep things running smoothly," I said.

"Don't be so modest. You're easy to talk to."

"She said something similar. I just listen. Without judging."

"She's the daughter I could never give you."

I hesitated. Then said, "Let's not distort the relationship, my dear. I didn't want kids any more than you did. Had enough of them at the university, boys and girls."

"Don't I know."

"And it affects me. I feel like now I'm dealing with her sadness."

"That's the price of empathy, accepting someone else's distress drops it on your lap."

"Wise observation, my dear. Let's talk about something more positive. Let's talk about love."

"Oh tell me about love, great sage."

"Forget it."

"No, I'm serious. I'd like to hear what you think."

"Well, it's not exactly positive. I think there's this huge element of fantasy involved. Good fantasy, but fantasy nonetheless. For instance, look at Melanie. She had built this world around a guy who treated her like shit. Cheating, lying, acting jealous, I'm sure there were fun moments, but in general it sounds like a horror show. She looks back now, sees how poorly George treated her, but why was she so easily fooled at the time?"

"Why?"

"Her ego fed her what she needed in order to keep going. That's the fantasy part. The mind misrepresents the reality in order to remain stable, to continue living under a pretense. You project what your lover feels, or doesn't feel about you. It's an inaccurate portrayal of what he really feels. You rationalize the negatives, or repress them."

"Are you fooling me?" Sarah asked.

"All the time. My words of love are carried on silver-tipped lies."

"I believe the word is tongue."

"Silver-tongued lies. For you."

"I get wet just listening to your words of love. Please lie to me some more."

"You'll have to come home. I can only lie when staring you in the face."

"I'll be on the next train," she said. "At any rate, I hope Melanie can bounce back."

"She's a strong woman," I said. "But even the strong can get knocked over. I often wonder if her hurt stems as much from the fact that she was dumped by such a loser."

"Interesting concept."

"Think about it. She's got everything going for her. George is rich but really just a family carpetbagger, taking what was for the giving. Wealth created by a previous generation. No character. And he dumps her."

"It happens."

"It's odd seeing a person with so much potential so doubtful about herself. Mel doesn't even see how much Johnny likes her, seemed surprised when I told her that."

"She'll emerge stronger," Sarah said. "She just needs friendships like yours."

I could never have predicted how true those words would bear out.

29

"Why here?" I asked.

"To wait." Melanie's reply was curt, almost indifferent. Her detachment surprised me. It was unlike her.

"Near Conner's Cliff?"

She nodded, backing the van into a small drive off the main road. She had called me early that morning to ask for help. Surprised at Melanie asking for help with anything, I immediately agreed to meet her at the brewery.

"What's going on?" I asked.

"I have to do something. I hope you'll back me."

"You know I will. But why so mysterious?"

"The less you know the better."

"Are you okay?"

"I'm fine. Just back me. Please." She looked at her phone, then back up the road from where we had come. The early morning hour and a light fog slightly obscured vision through the light rain that fell. "Should be coming any time."

"Do you plan to do something?" I was still mystified.

Melanie put her finger to her lips. I had never seen her so resolute.

I couldn't be silent. "I'm surprised you asked me for help."

"What do you mean?"

"You're a new breed of woman."

That got her attention.

"I mean with the growing opportunities for women, those your age sometimes overcompensate with self-reliance is all. I see more women trying to do everything without help."

"Look where dependence got us." She glanced back up the road again.

"It's not a criticism, just an observation."

"My dad taught me self-reliance."

"Like changing your own car's oil?"

She smiled. "Among other things."

"Must make it hard on relationships," I said.

"Most men can't deal with it," Melanie admitted. "They need that control."

"I'm not sure it's just control. We all want to feel needed."

"You really don't remember, do you."

"Remember what?"

She shook her head. "It's been bothering me since you said it. You don't remember him being in the courtroom."

I thought for a moment.

"He was there. It's why I left. I saw him."

It dawned on me what she was talking about. "Maybe I had already taken attendance?"

"Mine was perfect until that day."

We sat silently for a while. "I never missed your class," she said.

"I'm sorry... I mean, I'm flattered." I thought back to the courtroom scene. "I guess the memory that stands out that day is Brinkworth's breakdown. I can only remember one big thing at a time."

"It was the only time all semester that I missed your class. I couldn't even talk to you about it."

"So he *was* there."

She nodded, then glanced quickly at the road. "I found out more, too."

"About..."

"My mole told me he overheard the two of them talking in their office. It's not sound proof and he's a snooper."

"What did he hear?"

"Said they were talking about a skylight doing the job for them."

Open-mouthed, I turned to Melanie. She was looking up the road. "There it is."

She put the van into gear, pulled onto the road and stepped on the gas pedal.

The van sped up, but our acceleration wasn't quick enough. A horn sounded loudly and the truck veered to the left, pulled even with us. Melanie kept the van in our lane and pushed the pedal to the floor. Given the smaller size of the van and no load, we were able to equal the truck's speed. I glanced over to see the driver lift his middle finger at us and shout something. The artwork on the side of the truck loomed, the words at the bottom read Wehrmann & Sons.

Melanie kept her foot to the floor and we slowly pulled ahead. The horn sounded behind us again. Headlights flashed. The truck swerved recklessly back into our lane, behind us. Melanie increased our speed pulling away from the truck. The truck driver tried to close the gap, but Melanie had the advantage and kept us ahead of the racing vehicle.

I found myself admiring her driving skill. She had performed the entire maneuver without skidding on the slick road surface. Then I remembered.

"Conner's Cliff is up ahead. We'll never make the turn."

"I'm counting on it."

I glanced at her. She had an almost glazed look on her face, pure concentration.

The driver behind us hit the horn again, flashed the truck's headlights. Fifty feet before the curve, Melanie hit the brakes and swerved into the left lane. The truck, still speeding, pulled even.

"Close your eyes!" she yelled.

I did. And was thrown forward, then against the passenger side door, my neck coming up against the seat belt. My eyes snapped open and I watched the truck race ahead of us, straight toward the guard rail. Its brake lights were lit but there would be no stopping at this speed, on this road. Just before it hit the rail, the truck shuddered, then disappeared over the edge. Quiet descended, the silence of death.

30

Before beginning to swim, I usually oriented myself. It began with a locker room dose of local politics courtesy of the neighborhood seniors. So prepared, I'd enter the pool area and greet the lifeguards with a nod. I knew them by face rather than name because they passed through the job too quickly, on their way to college or full time work elsewhere. Then, assessing the pool's occupants, I would choose the most isolated lane.

Water temperature and clarity came next. Temperature was generally stable unless the twenty-plus year old system was malfunctioning, an occasional occurrence. Water clarity varied only slightly, just enough to give the seniors something to discuss. Water temperature and clarity were the weather talk of the senior swim regulars.

After noting the physical factors, I'd choose a lane, don my goggles and settle into a lap rhythm. Thoughts around the physical attributes would fade as I entered a solitary existence, reviewing concerns large and small. Swimming offered mental clarity.

This morning I hadn't even entered the pool area before my mind began churning over earlier events. Nodding at the seniors and neglecting to greet the lifeguards, I chose the lane furthest from the locker room door and swam, oblivious to my surroundings.

After the Wehrmann truck had disappeared over the cliff, Melanie stopped the van and started shaking, tears running down her face. I sat stunned. Suddenly, what Nate had written emerged from my subconscious: You are the quarterback, the leader. Callahans is yours to shepherd.

"I'll take the wheel." I got out of the van and called 911. Melanie said nothing, sitting motionless. I opened the driver's door and motioned for her to move over.

An officer arrived within minutes to take my statement. I told him I'd been driving, training my new driver on the morning route when the speeding truck tried to pass us and couldn't navigate the curve in the slippery conditions. He commented that speeding wasn't unusual here. I told him we had deliveries to make and asked permission to leave. The officer agreed, not bothering to look in the van, which held no cargo.

I turned at the pool's end and pushed off with the same measured strength I'd been using since beginning to swim. The water felt warm, appeared clearer than usual.

I had taken Melanie home. She appeared to be in a state of shock. Neither of us spoke.

Her head came up once we reached her apartment complex. "I'm sorry."

"For what?"

"I shouldn't have dragged you into this. It was my fight."

"I'm surprised you sought help. Like I said before, you seem to not want to rely on anyone."

She shrugged noncommittally.

"It's a good thing to ask for help," I continued. "No one's an island although sometimes we feel that way."

"I had to do it," she began. "If I was going to continue to live here, to work here. I..."

"You did what you had to do," I cut her off. "You should get some rest."

"I need a hot shower." She got out of the van.

"I'll make sure your car gets home. Take the rest of the day off if you need it."

"I don't want to be alone today. Besides, Stan's returning. We have to decorate the office."

"I have that covered."

"I want to help."

"Do you want me to wait while you get ready?"

"No, I'll be okay."

"Should I pick you up?"

"I'll call Johnny. He won't be riding his bike in this weather."

I left after watching her key herself into the apartment building's front door.

I turned, beginning another lap. I wondered what the police would find at the bottom of the cliff. Had Tony

Wehrmann been thrown out of the vehicle? Would they find cocaine in the truck? Would they test his body for foreign substances? I imagined someone reaching the truck after we'd left to hear him spit out some dying, incriminating words.

I didn't see how they could find anything to link us to the accident. Melanie's driving skill had kept us from touching the Wehrmann truck, a feat that still amazed me, and no cars had passed. Granted, my mind had been somewhat preoccupied, but anyone witnessing the scene would have stopped. How else could they connect us? Why wouldn't the police do what they'd done with Stan's running off the road and rule it an accident? The corner was a known hazard.

While the last few months had proven that I wasn't much of a detective, I still had questions. I thought about the connections. Accepting Melanie's claim that she had gone to court that morning, then left, what did that mean? Had Tony Wehrmann been involved in illegal toxic dumping? And how had I missed his presence in court?

Was the information Melanie fed me about the Wehrmann conversation even true? She had never identified her source beyond some guy with a crush on her and it was the only link I had between the landfill case, the distributor, and Brinkworth's death. Had she made it up to enlist my help?

Turning again, my thoughts shifted to Brinkworth and the gun he held when he fell to his death. What I recalled from our brief association was that his actions in court had threatened to expose an industry with purported links to larger crime. Our research at the university had revealed that some of the companies disposing of waste had questionable back-rounds, but we hadn't pursued the issue, preferring to insinuate a connection while hoping the state environmental agency would do the rest. Nothing had come of the information once the headlines disappeared.

As for Brinkworth, Jenna had worried that there would be expensive legal costs. She feared a lawsuit, a fear that wasn't entirely misplaced. The dead man had access to our ladder and the skylight was not sufficiently protected from "roof-wanderers," a term Mo used and said he planned to design a beer around.

It turned out that Randall Brinkworth had no living relatives. He had been a true loner. They found over one hundred growlers in his apartment, empty and unused. He'd also collected beer coasters, had some that would enthrall breweriana collectors.

With the possibility of a lawsuit over Brinkworth's death evaporating, we felt relieved. Mo began to talk about building on the Dead Lawyer image, creating an icon to help market our beer. Roof Wanderer, Skylight Jumper, Growler Grinch, his mind never stopped.

Finishing my swim, I congratulated myself on another mile. Sticking to a regimen helped keep my motivation high. I also felt congratulations were due for my stepping into the leadership role after the accident. It hadn't come naturally, but was a step in that direction. Regardless of what happened, I felt good.

I remembered an incident from Nate's past, his last year of high school. His team had been near the end of a championship game against a stronger squad. They had kept the team to less than a touchdown margin, a worthy feat. He'd come off the field exhausted. The entire team was exhausted. They had held their own against a better team. But their opponents had regained the ball.

Our coach knew he'd pushed the boys as far as he could. Seeing the tired huddle around him, he asked who wanted to go onto the field to try to hold their opponents to a respectable margin. Nate had raised his hand immediately. From my position on the nearby bleachers I could see that he hardly had the energy to keep his hand raised. Several of his teammates took inspiration from him and volunteered.

The opposing team's arrogance ruined them. Instead of running out the clock, they moved toward another touchdown. The quarterback fumbled the ball and Nate scooped it up and ran into the end zone. He'd walked away with another trophy, a hero again.

That evening I asked him why he had volunteered. He said his hand had gone up automatically. "Somebody had to do it," was all he said.

31

"You okay?"

Melanie smiled. "I haven't felt this good in years."

"It's good to see you smile." We sat in the brewery office, about to decorate it.

"How about you? Are you okay with it all?"

"I'm fine," I said.

"Fine as in 'I'll live with what happened,' or fine as in, 'I'm glad about what happened?'"

I laughed. Her concern for me boded well. "I still haven't processed it all, but at any moment I could have stopped you." I hesitated. "Well, maybe not."

"Have you told anyone?"

"Not yet."

"Are you going to?"

"I haven't had time to think that over. Sarah..."

"Sarah won't think it was fine."

"She knows what he did to you."

Melanie remained silent.

"You're asking me to keep this a secret?" I asked.

"You're probably not used to that. Keeping secrets."

"Let me think on it. I won't tell anyone before I alert you. Meanwhile, let's get these decorations up."

"What can I do?"

I handed her several rolls of stretch paper. Today was a big day and we wanted to welcome Stan's return in style. It had been Sarah's idea, of course, a female touch to my nuts and bolts approach. While I worried about where to put our returning sales chief and owner in the office, and how to split up the sale accounts, Sarah forced me to simply stop and celebrate.

"What do you think of Mo's newest beer?" Melanie asked, once we'd begun decorating.

"Which one is that?"

"The sage IPA."

"You've had it?"

"He gave me a taste from Oscar."

"I haven't tasted it yet," I said. "What did you think?"

"I like it, but I like everything he brews. The sage is pretty aggressive. I wonder how it will sell to Calla-Fans."

Melanie had learned quite a bit in the months she'd worked at Callahans. Indicative of this was her re-focusing on the customer base. While she may prefer a beer, it was the customer that decided. This countered Mo's intention to challenge every taste bud on earth.

Mel's change in focus had led her to the ingenious idea of the Calla-Fan Club. She'd created the group from our regular customers by offering special discounts and pre-release tastings of Mo's beers in exchange for a yearly fee. The club was such a hit that we'd had to limit it to one hundred people. A waiting list for new Calla-Fans was created, with spots opening once a year, from members who didn't renew.

In addition to creating loyalty, we used the Calla-Fan Club to gauge Mo's latest creations. A combination of what they liked and what we preferred gave us better feedback on what would sell.

"We'll be doing a comparison tasting next week to give Mo some feedback."

"I'm not sure there's much to compare a sage IPA to," I said. "I mean, how many sage-flavored beers do you know about, especially when it's used in place of hops?"

"I did some research and could only find one brewery that had done a sage-hopped beer."

"California?"

"Michigan. A brewpub."

I couldn't believe what a beer geek Melanie was. "By the way, the Calla-Fan Club was a great idea. You deserve a lot of credit."

"Thank you."

"The annual renewal is smart, brings in money right when we hit our January sales lull."

"I didn't think of that, but I'm glad it helps." She tacked up the last of the streamers. "I love working here."

Melanie's comment couldn't have made me any prouder.

"Got a minute?" she asked. "I want to show you something."

I followed her out of the office and behind the horizontals, where she retrieved a large plastic bag. Removing the bag revealed a dry erase board with vertical and horizontal lines drawn to create a grid. Down the side, spaced evenly, were three names: Stan, Melanie, and Ed. Along the top were names of the bars where we sold our beer.

"Reminds me of the university," I said.

"I liked the way you displayed progress openly in the classroom. That way we could keep an eye out for what we had done, and needed to do."

"That was an age before on-line updates."

"It also urged on the dark horses."

"Am I going to have to bring back the Dark Horse Report?"

"I think so."

"I'll have to regain my voice." At the university, at the end of each week, I had reviewed the progress reports with my classes, playing the horse race announcer and stoking the leaders while urging the laggards to become winners. I had developed a good race voice and the Dark Horse Report had become a favorite way to end my classes each Friday. It also kept attendance high on a day not normally known for it.

"I did it for Nate," Mel added, sounding apologetic. "He wanted us to grow. This board is easier, of course," she added. "It's only you, me, and if he's ready to get back into the race, Stan."

"Oh he'll be ready," I replied.

"Do you think he'll mind?"

"Mind? How many jocks have you known? The thought of competition makes them salivate. It's right up Stan's alley."

"Good."

"I only hope you don't start something you'll regret," I said.

"Is that a challenge?"

I heard noise outside. "I think they've arrived. Where's Johnny and Mo?"

"In the cooler. I'll get them."

The front door opened. Stan entered, wrestling with crutches while carrying a case of pint glasses. I took the case. "Stan, how are you?"

"Wheels are spinnin' even if they aren't completely healed."

"You look good."

"Doc says give it another month. Jenna's on his side, likes my Mister Mom role, but I need to get busy."

Outside, I saw Jenna reaching into the back seat to pull Junior out of his car seat. "Let me go help her. Sit down." I put a chair out for Stan, set the glasses on a nearby shelf and went outside.

Jenna turned when she heard me. "You'd think adults could figure these out!"

"I don't have much experience, but..." I couldn't help but notice. "You're..."

"Stan and I are expecting!" she said. "Junior is going to need a sibling."

"Wow!" was all I could manage. I bent into the car to figure out the release on the car seat and looked—as if for the first time—at Junior. And saw the resemblance. How could I have missed it? A lot of people confused Nate and Stan when they first met them, said they looked like twins, but to family or anyone familiar with the two, the differences were obvious. The shape of their noses was different and Nate's eyes were narrow and wide while Stan's were round. Whatever the similarities and differences, it was good to have Stan back.

"How do things look?" I asked, once I had Junior free from his seat.

"Great!" she replied.

"The business?"

"The business is good."

"So we're out of the woods financially."

"I replenished the emergency account. A couple of payments from fly-by-nights fearing notification of the state liquor authority helped."

"I've always liked that law."

"The account is back up where it should be. I feel good about it."

I must have looked shocked, because Jenna added, "Nate told me you reacted well to urgency. That you were a sink or swim kind of guy."

"Hence the dire warnings."

"Yes."

"It worked." I smiled.

"You're a different man since then. Seem more focused, strong."

Strong like the industry to which I now belonged. Nate had marveled at this strength, in fact said it was one of the things that most attracted him to brewing. For me, it was invigorating compared to the university. Granted, the infighting I'd experienced was as much about the naming of the Chemistry building as characteristic of the profession, but the divisions had spoiled the job for me. We had fought a losing battle of principle, watching our righteous cause dissolve into pettiness as the administration and its adherents rammed their agenda through.

How rewarding to work in an industry where differences were celebrated. Small breweries worked together and found strength in that union. We overlooked the loss of a knob to a competitor if it meant a gain for the whole because the potential for gain was bigger if we stuck together. One thing we had gotten right was to see that the real competition came from the larger, national brands.

I remembered something Melanie said when I'd first hired her. "When I was with George, we would go to a bar and he would count knobs. The beer meant nothing to him and he would frown when I complimented a beer they didn't distribute. He just saw the knobs, didn't care about the beer. It was all about whether his company distributed it. Essentially, I came to realize that I was about the beer and he was about the business."

It reminded me of the similar conversation I'd had with Nate. "It's a good match to have," I had commented at the time.

"But they're only about the business. They're blind to what the beer is. I mean, they know something about it, but they have no appreciation beyond price point and access. It could be piss water, it doesn't matter. He actually said that to me more than once."

By the time I had gotten Junior into the building, the rest of the staff had gathered in the office. They sat wearing party hats and holding noise makers. Mo had popped a celebratory beer, a sour that he'd test brewed on his home system. He called it a stovetop sour.

Stan was gazing at the sales board. "Do I get a handicap?"

"If you don't think you can hack it," Mel replied.

"What..."

Again I felt pride at my new hire. "Damn, Stan, you are in for some real competition."

"Can't wait," he replied. "How we gonna deal with the accounts I sold and you two maintained?"

"Maybe we can give half of those to Ed," Mel said. "He's gonna need a few so his sales don't look too dismal."

"Ow," I said.

"I think I like this new girl," Stan said.

"Woman to you," Johnny said. I looked at our keg monkey, surprised.

"And you are the legend." Melanie stepped forward to shake Stan's hand.

"You'll have to apologize for the weak grip. Still not up to full strength."

I swirled the beer in my glass and smelled the lovely, acidic aroma, not quite Belgian, but on its way. "Mel is opening up new accounts and I've been covering yours. I never knew how much work it was. I'm still not sure how to divide up the work load."

A thought occurred to me, another observation Nate had made. Most people didn't realize the stamina in a human body was far greater than we gave it credit for. It's why he had excelled on the sports field. At the point where most players were exhausted, he would reach into himself and find more, make his move.

It would be smart to remember this, I thought, as I surveyed my crew. There would be trials. But I had in front of me people who showed the knowledge and enthusiasm to compete on any field. They had large reserves of strength. I could sense the stamina that Nate spoke about. We had what it took to carry Callahans to the next level.

ABOUT THE AUTHOR

Bill Metzger began writing and editing for a bimonthly magazine, Central New York Environment, in 1980. Since then he has written humor and travel pieces based on traveling with a loosely knit group of international beer tasters, *Los Testigos de Cerveza*. His travels have been catalogued in numerous beer-focused publications, including American Brewer, The New Brewer, and Yankee Brew News.

In 1992, Bill created *Southwest Brewing News*, a consumer-based, bi-monthly publication about the microbrewing industry. Since then he has grown Brewing News to encompass eight newspapers covering the United States and Canada.

CPSIA information can be obtained
at www.ICGtesting.com
Printed in the USA
FFOW05n1028080216

9 781609 751357